A Time to Laugh

Also edited by Sara and Stephen Corrin

THE FABER BOOK OF CHRISTMAS STORIES
ROUND THE CHRISTMAS TREE
ONCE UPON A RHYME: 101 Poems for Young Children
THE FABER BOOK OF MODERN FAIRY TALES
STORIES FOR UNDER-FIVES
STORIES FOR FIVE-YEAR-OLDS
STORIES FOR SIX-YEAR-OLDS
STORIES FOR SEVEN-YEAR-OLDS
MORE STORIES FOR SEVEN-YEAR-OLDS
STORIES FOR EIGHT-YEAR-OLDS
STORIES FOR NINE-YEAR-OLDS
STORIES FOR TENS AND OVER

retold by Sara and Stephen Corrin
Illustrated by Errol Le Cain
MRS FOX'S WEDDING

ff

A TIME TO LAUGH

Edited by Sara & Stephen Corrin

Funny Stories for Children
Illustrated by Gerald Rose

faber and faber
LONDON · BOSTON

First published in 1972
by Faber and Faber Limited
3 Queen Square London WC1N 3AU
Faber Fanfares edition 1980
First published in this edition 1985

Printed in Great Britain by
Whitstable Litho Ltd., Whitstable, Kent
All rights reserved

British Library Cataloguing in Publication Data

Corrin, Sara
A time to laugh.
1. Children's stories, English
I. Title   II. Corrin, Stephen
823'.01'089282 [J] PZ5
ISBN 0-571-13416-5

Contents

Contents

Contents

Acknowledgements

❖

We are most grateful to the undermentioned publishers, authors and agents for permission to include the following stories:

Abelard-Schuman for *The Emperor's Oblong Pancake* by Peter Hughes.

André Deutsch Limited for *The Ugsome Thing* from *Ten Tales of Shellover* by Ruth Ainsworth.

Evans Brothers (Books) Limited for *The Wishing-skin* from *Ten Minute Tales* by Rhoda Power.

Blackie and Son Limited for *Clever Oonagh* from *Fairy Tales from the British Isles* by Amabel Williams-Ellis.

Hutchinson Publishing Group Limited for *Mrs. Pepperpot Buys Macaroni* from *Little Old Mrs. Pepperpot* by Alf Proysen.

William Heinemann Limited for *The Ju-Ju Man* from *Cherry Stones* by Ruth Ainsworth.

Chatto and Windus Limited for *The Elephant's Picnic* from *Don't Blame Me* by Richard Hughes.

Barrie and Jenkins Limited for *A Meal with a Magician* from *My Friend Mr. Leakey* by J. B. S. Haldane.

Hodder and Stoughton Children's Books (formerly Brockhampton Press Ltd) for *The Woman Who Always Argued* by Leila Berg.

Mrs. George Bambridge and Macmillan and Co. for *The Elephant's Child* from *Just So Stories* by Rudyard Kipling.

The Estate of A. A. Milne and Curtis Brown Limited for *Eeyore Loses a Tail and Pooh Finds One* from *Winnie the Pooh* by A. A. Milne.

Acknowledgements

The E. Nesbit Estate and John Farquharson Limited for *The Magician's Heart* by E. Nesbit.

David Higham Associates Limited for *Can Men Be Such Fools as All That?* by Eleanor Farjeon.

Blackie and Son Limited for *The Chatterbox* by Amabel Williams-Ellis and Moura Budberg.

ABP International for *Puss and Pup* from *Harum Scarum* by J. Čapek.

We should like to thank Mrs. S. Stonebridge, Principal Children's Librarian, Royal Borough of Kensington and Chelsea, Mrs. Mary Clunes, Children's Librarian, Golders Green Public Library, Hazel Wilkinson, Mary Junor, Schools Librarian, Barnet, and Eileen Leach, Children's Librarian, Watford Library; for their ever-willing and invaluable help and advice; and, of course, Phyllis Hunt of Faber and Faber for constant guidance and encouragement.

Introduction

◆

What do children laugh at? Although as adults we tend to think that their sense of humour is cruder and simpler than ours, closer analysis suggests that the basic stuff of humour is the same for child and man alike: the little man outwitting the braggart and bully; the supercilious and haughty brought to justice; the theme of 'the smile on the face of the tiger'; slapstick; sweet revenge, as in *The Fox and the Stork* and the Tar-Baby stories; ingratitude punished by elegant cunning, as in *The Tiger, the Brahmin and the Jackal*; the victim of the heavy hand of authority hitting back, as when the Elephant's Child spanks all his relatives with his newly-found trunk. Nothing delights children more than the moment when he picks up his hairy uncle, the baboon, by one hairy leg and throws him into a hornet's nest.

The nagging wife theme, recurrent in folktale, where the woman receives her just deserts, is sometimes counterbalanced in other tales when the wife becomes the heroine, her cunning and wit helping her husband out of a scrape. Incongruity is a source of humour: the diminutive Mrs. Pepperpot mistaken for a mouse by the embarrassed shopkeeper who adopts comic means to cover up his discomfiture. So is the theme of the woman with the patience of a Job who turns the tables on her tormentor, as in *The Ugsome Thing*.

The appeal to the child's rough sense of justice finds a never-failing response. The preposterous antics of Little Claus, robbed by his powerful neighbour of his only means of livelihood, are accepted in spite of their outrageous improbability. The brave little tailor illustrates the dream of the weak becoming stout-hearted and reflects, perhaps, the fantasies of the child in his play when he sees himself as the King of the Castle.

Such is the stuff these tales are made of and such is the stuff that has made them survive.

Clever Oonagh

♦

There was once a giant in Ireland called Cucullin, and another giant that was also supposed to be a mighty warrior, though he wasn't near so big. His name was Fin. There's many a terrible tale told about these two—Cucullin and Fin—and their great and famous deeds and their battles. But there's one story about them and about Fin's wife, Oonagh, which is different. Maybe it's just a tale that was told round about the country by those who were sick and tired of hearing only about their killing and slaughtering and the great deeds. Perhaps a few people wanted to have the laugh of them.

Now Fin had his house at the very top of a steep hill called Knockmany, which wasn't really just such a very convenient place for a house, because, you see, whichever way the wind blew, it always blew up there. Another thing was that, when her husband Fin was away, Oonagh had always to go down to the very bottom of the steep hill to the spring before she could draw a drop of water, and then she had to carry her full pails all the way to the top again.

But all the same 'twas a good spot for a house in one way, for being perched up like that at the very top of Knockmany Hill, Fin could see all ways—North, South, East and West—and that gave him a good warning if any of his enemies should take it into their heads to pay him a visit. Fin wasn't one to like being taken by surprise. He had yet another way of getting a warning, as well as keeping a good look-out. He would put his thumb into his mouth till it touched one special tooth, right at the back, and then the thumb would tell him what was coming to pass.

Well, one day, when all seemed peaceful, Fin was sitting with his wife, Oonagh, when she saw that he had put his thumb in his mouth.

"What are you doing that for, Fin?" says she.

"Oh, my grief and sorrow, he's coming!" said Fin as soon as he had pulled out his thumb and could speak plain, and she saw that he looked as miserable as a wet Sunday.

"Who's coming?" asked Oonagh.

"That horrid beast of an old Cucullin, no less," answered Fin.

Now, as Oonagh well knew, though Fin was near as tall and big as a round-tower, Cucullin was bigger still and was an enemy that Fin didn't want to meet, no not for all the world. All the giants for miles around were afraid of Cucullin. When he was angry and gave a stamp with his foot, the whole country shook. Once, by a blow of his fist, he had flattened a thunder-bolt till it was flat as a pancake, and ever after he kept it in his pocket to show to anyone who offered to fight with him. Fin was a match for most of the rest of the giants, and had even boasted that the great Cucullin had never—so far—come near him for fear he would get a drubbing. But now, oh grief and sorrow! Cucullin, no less, was on his way, and Fin didn't like the idea—no, not at all!

"How to get round such a terrible fellow, or what to do, I don't know," went on Fin to his wife in a very doleful tone. "If I run away while there's still time I shall be a laughing-stock to all the other giants, and a terrible disgrace will be on me. But how to fight with a giant that makes a pancake out of a thunder-bolt with one blow of his fist, and that shakes the whole country with one stamp of his foot, I don't know!"

"How far has he got?" asks Oonagh.

"As far as Dungannon," answers Fin.

"How soon will he be here?" asks she.

"Tomorrow about two o'clock," answers he, and then he adds with a groan, "And meet him I shall for my thumb tells me so."

" Now, now, my dear! Don't fret and don't be cast down!" answers Oonagh. "Let's see if I can't be the one to bring you out of your great trouble!"

"For the love of all the saints, Oonagh my darling, do what you can! Else for sure I'll either be skinned like a rabbit before your eyes, or else have my name disgraced before the whole tribe of giants. Oh, my grief! Oh, my sorrow! If this isn't just a regular earthquake of a fellow, and him with a pancake in his pocket that was once a thunderbolt!"

"For shame on you, Fin! Be easy now! Pancake, did you say? See now if I can't treat that bully boy to some feeding that'll give him a sore tooth! Leave your moaning and lamenting now, Fin! If I can't get around and circumvent that great lump of a fellow, never trust Oonagh again."

With that she went to where her skeins of wool were hung out to dry after she had dyed them and she took nine long strands of all the colours she had. She plaited the wool-threads three and three, and when it was done she tied one plait round her right arm, one round her right ankle and the third and longest she tied right round her, over her heart.

She'd done all this several times before, when Fin was in trouble, so his mind got a bit firmer when he saw what she was at, for the truth is she hadn't ever failed yet when she had got the threads on her.

"Is there time for me to go round to the neighbours?" Oonagh asked.

"There is time," said Fin. So off she set and she went to this one and that. When she came back Fin saw that she had borrowed a whole load of griddles—which are thin irons, like huge plates, for making scones or flat bread over a turf fire. Then he saw how she kneaded enough dough to make as many griddle loaves as she had irons. One she cooked in the proper way and made a good round flat loaf of it—as big as a cart-wheel nearly —but all the rest were made in a very strange way, for she made them two-sided each with an iron griddle hidden in the middle. As each one was done, she put it away in the bread-cupboard. Then she made a big milk cheese and she boiled a whole side of bacon, set it to cool, and began to boil a sackful of cabbages.

By this time it was evening, the evening of the day before Cucullin was to come, and the last thing Oonagh did was to light a high smoking bonfire on the hill outside and to put her fingers in her mouth to give three whistles. This was to let Cucullin know that strangers were invited to Knockmany, for that was the way that the Irish, long ago, would be giving a sign to travellers that they could come in. Oonagh didn't tell Fin about her plans that night, but she did ask him a few things about Cucullin, and one of the things that Fin told her was that Cucullin's mighty strength lay in just the one place, and that was the middle finger of his right hand.

Next morning, as you can guess, Fin was on the look-out, and after a while he saw how his enemy Cucullin—as tall as a church tower—was striding along across the valley.

Back into the house went Fin and his face was as white as Oonagh's milk cheese when he was telling her the news. But Oonagh only smiled, she had something ready for Fin too.

"Now Fin dear! Take it more easy! Be guided by me. Here's the cradle that the children are too old for now, and here's a white bonnet, and here's a nightgown of mine that will look for all the world like a baby's robe when you have it on over your shirt. Dress yourself up, lie down snug in the cradle, and cover yourself with the quilt, say nothing, and be guided by me, for this day you must pass for your own child."

Fin was shaking with fear and he was scarcely tucked up, when there came a regular thunder of a knock on the door.

"Come in and welcome!" cried Oonagh, and, with that, a great huge man twice as big as old Fin, opened the door. And

16

who was it but the mighty Cucullin himself, as punctual to his time as the stars themselves.

"God save all here," says he in a great rumbling voice. "And is this where the famous Fin lives?"

"Indeed and it is! Come in and rest, honest man."

"It's Mrs. Fin you'll be?" says he, coming in and sitting down.

"Indeed and I am, and a fine strong husband I have," says she.

"Aye," says he, "he has the name of being one of the best giants in Ireland, but all the same there's one come that is very willing to try to get the better of him in a fair fight."

"Dear me!" says Oonagh. "Isn't that a grievous pity now, for he left the house in a fury this very morning at the first light. Word had come that a great big bully of a giant by the name of Cucullin had gone down to look for him on the northern coast of the sea—the place where the Irish giants are building their causeway to get to Scotland. Saints above! But I hope for the poor ignorant fellow's sake that he doesn't find Fin, for Fin'll make paste of Cucullin this day, he's in such a fury!"

"It's I am Cucullin, and it's I that am after fighting with Fin!" answered Cucullin, frowning. "This twelve-month I'm after looking for him, and it's Fin that will be ground to paste, not me!"

"My sorrow! I'm thinking that you never saw Fin," said Oonagh, shaking her head.

"How could I see Fin," answered Cucullin, "and him dodging all the while to get away from me like as if he was a snipe on a bog?"

"Fin dodging to get away from you, is it, you poor little creature?" says Oonagh. "I tell you it'll be the black day for you if ever you do see Fin, and let's only hope the wild furious temper that is on him now will have cooled a bit, or else it's rushing to your death you'd be. Rest here a while and when you go it's me that will pray to the holy saints that you never catch up with Fin.''

Cucullin began to wonder a bit about such words, so he didn't speak for a while, and presently Oonagh said, looking about her:

"Isn't that just a terrible wind that's blowing in at the door and making the smoke come down! Fin always helps me when it does that. As he's from home, perhaps you'd be civil enough to do the job for me?"

"What job is that?" asked Cucullin.

"Oh, just to turn the house round for me. That's what Fin always does."

This made Cucullin wonder a bit more. However, he got up and then Oonagh noticed, that as he stood there he pulled at the middle finger of his right hand till it gave three little cracks, and she remembered how Fin had told her that it was in this finger that Cucullin's mighty strength lay.

Well, after that he stumped outside on his great legs, put his two great arms round the house and turned it round, just as Oonagh had asked him to do.

Fin, hiding in the cradle, felt ready to die with fear to see the like of that, for of course he never had turned the house for Oonagh, no, not in all the long time they'd been married.

But Oonagh, who was outside with Cucullin, gave a sweet smile and a plain 'thank you', making out that turning a whole house round was as easy as opening a door.

"Since you're so civil, perhaps you'd do another obliging thing for me, Fin being away," says she.

"What obliging thing is that?" asked Cucullin.

"Nothing very great," says she. "But after this spell of dry weather we've been after enduring, I'm having to go down the hill for every drop of water. Only last night Fin promised me he'd get at a spring of water there is under the rocks at the back. But he left home in such a temper, chasing after you to fight you, that he forgot all about it. I'll have a bite of dinner ready for you, if you'll just pull the rocks asunder for me."

So she brought Cucullin down to see the place, and indeed it was all rock and part of the mountain itself, with only one small crack in it, so that you could scarcely hear the water gurgling underneath.

It was plain from the look on Cucullin's face that he didn't like the job. However, he pulled his finger three times and took another look, then he pulled it three times again, and had another look, and still he didn't like what he saw, for the job was no less than to rend the mountain itself.

However, after he had pulled his finger yet three times more —that was nine times in all—he stepped down. This time he tore a great cleft in the side of the mountain, and it was four hundred feet deep and half a mile long. (It's there to this day —Lumford's Glen they call it.)

"That's very obliging of you I'm sure," says Oonagh. "And now away back to the house, for you to get a bite of dinner, for Fin would be blaming me if I let you go without, even if you are enemies, and even if it's only our own humble fare that I can set before you."

Fin, you remember, was still in the cradle, and hadn't seen what had been going on outside, but all the same he was quaking and shivering to see Cucullin coming back with Oonagh and sitting down at the table.

Oonagh served the giant with two big cans of butter, the whole side of bacon, and she had the whole sack of cabbages ready boiled for him. Last of all she brought out a pile of the big round flat loaves that she had baked the day before.

"Help yourself, and welcome," says she.

So Cucullin started on the bacon and cabbages and then he picked up one of the big flat loaves and opened his mouth wide to take a huge bite out of it. But he had scarcely bitten into that bread before he let out a terrible yell.

"Blood and fury!" cries he.

"What's the matter?" asks Oonagh.

"Matter enough!" cries he. "Here's two of my best teeth

cracked. What kind of bread is this?"

"Why," said Oonagh, making out that she was very much surprised, "that's only Fin's bread! Even his child in the cradle there can eat it!" With that she took the one flat loaf that hadn't got a griddle inside it, and she went across to Fin where he lay in the cradle, and gave him the bread and a hard nudge.

Cucullin watched, and sure enough the thing in the cradle took a huge bite out of the bread and then started munching.

"Here's another loaf for you, Cucullin!" says Oonagh, shaking her head as if she pitied him. "Maybe this one'll be softer for you."

But this one had a griddle inside it as well, and when he tried to bite it Cucullin let out a yell that was louder than the first, for he'd bitten harder, not liking the way Oonagh had seemed to pity him.

This yell of Cucullin's was so loud that it frightened Fin into letting out a yell as well.

"There now, you've gone and upset the child!" says Oonagh. "If you're not able to eat Fin's bread, why can't you say so quietly?"

But Cucullin hadn't got an answer to that, for he was beginning to feel a bit frightened. What with turning the house, and what with tearing up the mountain, and now what with seeing Fin's child, though it was still in its cradle, munching that terrible bread before his very eyes, he was beginning to think that it really was a good thing he hadn't found Fin at home. Maybe all that Oonagh had been telling him was nothing but the truth!

"And is it special teeth they all have in Fin's family?" asked Cucullin at last, nursing his own jaw. His mouth was too sore for any more bacon and cabbage.

"Would you like to feel for yourself?" answered Oonagh. "I'll get the little fellow to open his mouth for you. But perhaps you'd be afraid of him? It's rather far back in his mouth his teeth are—just put in your longest finger!"

Well, can you guess now what happened? Indeed perhaps you'd hardly believe it, if you didn't know already that there's hardly an end to the foolishness of giants. Yes, that was it!

Cucullin, with a little bit of help from Oonagh, was so foolish as to put in that one special finger of his, the middle finger of his right hand, right into Fin's mouth! Well, maybe Fin wasn't the bravest or the wisest, but all the same he was wise enough to give a good hard bite when he had such a chance as that! So now there stood Cucullin without his finger, and worse than that, without his strength. So at last, Fin plucked up his courage, jumped out of the cradle and then Cucullin thought best to run for it.

Away and away, all down Knockmany Hill Fin chased him, for if Cucullin's strength was gone, he could still run. So at last, since he couldn't catch him Fin came back, and by then Oonagh had taken the griddles out of the loaves. So the two of them sat down in peace to eat what was left of the dinner that clever Oonagh had set for Cucullin.

Mrs. Pepperpot Buys Macaroni

◇

"It's a very long time since we've had macaroni for supper," said Mr. Pepperpot one day.

"Then you shall have it today, my love," said his wife. "But I shall have to go to the grocer for some. So first of all you'll have to find me."

"Find you?" said Mr. Pepperpot. "What sort of nonsense is that?" But when he looked round for her he couldn't see her anywhere. "Don't be silly, wife," he said; "if you're hiding in the cupboard you must come out this minute. We're too big to play hide-and-seek."

"I'm not too big, I'm just the right size for 'hunt-the-pepperpot'," laughed Mrs. Pepperpot. "Find me if you can!"

"I'm not going to charge round my own bedroom looking for my wife," he said crossly.

"Now, now! I'll help you; I'll tell you when you're warm. Just now you're very cold." For Mr. Pepperpot was peering out of the window, thinking she might have jumped out. As he searched round the room she called out "Warm!", "Colder!", "Getting hotter!" until he was quite dizzy.

At last she shouted, "You'll burn the top of your bald head if you don't look up!" And there she was, sitting on the bed post, swinging her legs and laughing at him.

Her husband pulled a very long face when he saw her.

"This is a bad business—a very bad business," he said, stroking her cheek with his little finger.

"I don't think it's a bad business," said Mrs. Pepperpot.

"I shall have a terrible time. The whole town will laugh when they see I have a wife the size of a pepperpot."

"Who cares?" she answered. "That doesn't matter a bit. Now put me down on the floor so that I can get ready to go to the grocer and buy your macaroni."

But her husband wouldn't hear of her going; he would go to the grocer himself.

"That'll be a lot of use!" she said. "When you get home you'll have forgotten to buy the macaroni. I'm sure even if I wrote 'macaroni' right across your forehead you'd bring back cinnamon and salt herrings instead."

"But how are you going to walk all that way with those tiny legs?"

"Put me in your coat pocket; then I won't need to walk."

There was no help for it, so Mr. Pepperpot put his wife in his pocket and set off for the shop.

Soon she started talking: "My goodness me, what a lot of strange things you have in your pocket—screws and nails, tobacco and matches—there's even a fish-hook! You'll have to take that out at once; I might get it caught in my skirt."

"Don't talk so loud," said her husband as he took out the fish-hook. "We're going into the shop now."

It was an old-fashioned village store where they sold everything from prunes to coffee cups. The grocer was particularly proud of the coffee cups and held one up for Mr. Pepperpot to see. This made his wife curious and she popped her head out of his pocket.

"You stay where you are!" whispered Mr. Pepperpot.

"I beg your pardon, did you say anything?" asked the grocer.

"No, no, I was just humming a little tune," said Mr. Pepperpot. "Tra-la-la!"

"What colour are the cups?" whispered his wife. And her husband sang:

24

Mrs. Pepperpot Buys Macaroni

"The cups are blue
With gold edge too,
But they cost too much
So that won't do!"

After that Mrs. Pepperpot kept quiet—but not for long.
When her husband pulled out his tobacco tin she couldn't resist
hanging on to the lid. Neither her husband nor anyone else in
the shop noticed her slipping on to the counter and hiding
behind a flour-bag. From there she darted silently across to the
scales, crawled under them, past a pair of kippers wrapped in
newspaper, and found herself next to the coffee cups.

"Aren't they pretty!" she whispered, and took a step backwards to get a better view. Whoops! She fell right into the
macaroni drawer which had been left open. She hastily covered

herself up with macaroni, but the grocer heard the scratching noise and quickly banged the drawer shut. You see, it did sometimes happen that mice got in the drawers, and that's not the sort of thing you want people to know about, so the grocer pretended nothing had happened and went on serving.

There was Mrs. Pepperpot all in the dark; she could hear the grocer serving her husband now. "That's good," she thought. "When he orders macaroni I'll get my chance to slip into the bag with it."

But it was just as she had feared; her husband forgot what he had come to buy. Mrs. Pepperpot shouted at the top of her voice, "MACARONI!", but it was impossible to get him to hear.

"A quarter of a pound of coffee, please," said her husband.

"Anything else?" asked the grocer.

"MACARONI!" shouted Mrs. Pepperpot.

"Two pounds of sugar," said her husband.

"Anything more?"

"MACARONI!" shouted Mrs. Pepperpot.

But at last her husband remembered the macaroni of his own accord. The grocer hurriedly filled a bag. He thought he felt something move, but he didn't say a word.

"That's all, thank you," said Mr. Pepperpot. When he got outside the door he was just about to make sure his wife was still in his pocket when a van drew up and offered to give him a lift all the way home. Once there he took off his knapsack with all the shopping in it and put his hand in his pocket to lift out his wife.

The pocket was empty.

Now he was really frightened. First he thought she was teasing him, but when he had called three times and still no wife appeared, he put on his hat again and hurried back to the shop.

The grocer saw him coming. "He's probably going to complain about the mouse in the macaroni," he thought.

"Have you forgotten anything, Mr. Pepperpot?" he asked, and smiled as pleasantly as he could.

Mr. Pepperpot was looking all round. "Yes," he said.

"I would be very grateful, Mr. Pepperpot, if you would keep it to yourself about the mouse being in the macaroni. I'll let you have these fine blue coffee cups if you'll say no more about it."

"Mouse?" Mr. Pepperpot looked puzzled.

"Shh!" said the grocer, and hurriedly started wrapping up the cups.

Then Mr. Pepperpot realized that the grocer had mistaken his wife for a mouse. So he took the cups and rushed home as fast as he could. By the time he got there he was in a sweat of fear that his wife might have been squeezed to death in the macaroni bag.

"Oh, my dear wife," he muttered to himself. "My poor darling wife. I'll never again be ashamed of you being the size of a pepperpot—as long as you're still alive!"

When he opened the door she was standing by the cooking-stove, dishing up the macaroni—as large as life; in fact, as large as you or I.

The Emperor's Oblong Pancake

Long, long ago in the East there was an Emperor who loved pancakes. Every day of the year he had six pancakes for breakfast; great, big yellow ones they were, and a little bit brown on top; in fact, just done to a turn.

And, of course, they were round; as round as round as round.

One fine morning in spring, when all the almond trees in the palace courtyard were bursting into blossom, the Emperor came down to breakfast feeling especially merry. You see, it was his birthday.

"Happy Birthday, your Excellency," said the first footman, as the Emperor sat down at the breakfast table, and he pushed the Emperor's chair up snug behind his knees.

"Happy Birthday, your Excellency," said the second footman, as he laid out the Emperor's golden spoon, fork and knife in front of him.

"Happy Birthday, your Excellency," said the third footman, helping to tuck the Emperor's gleaming white napkin into his red velvet collar, and spreading it neatly over his gold-embroidered waistcoat.

"Happy Birthday, your Excellency," said the Court Chamberlain as he bowed low. Then he beckoned forward the first footman again, bearing a huge golden bowl full of hot, steaming porridge.

"And the same to you," said the Emperor, merrily, as he shook the sugar and poured the cream; and with that he set briskly to work, opening all his birthday cards with his left hand, and scooping porridge into his mouth with his right, as merry as merry could be.

In no time at all the Emperor's porridge was finished, and all his birthday cards were propped up in front of him. Immediately the third footman whisked away the empty plate, and the Court Chamberlain marched solemnly to the door, where he took up the big gong stick, made of solid ebony, and beat the big gong, made of solid brass. This was the signal for the fourth and fifth footmen to bring in the main dish.

At the far end of the dining room the big bronze doors flew open, and in came the fourth and fifth footmen, bearing between them a broad silver dish with a broad silver dish cover. Up the length of the dining room they marched, with the Court Chamberlain walking in front, carrying his wand of office until they reached the Emperor.

The fourth and fifth footmen bowed as low as low. "Happy Birthday, your Excellency," they cried together.

"And the same to you," beamed the Emperor, still as merry as ever, and he rubbed his hands together in anticipation, as the fourth and fifth footmen took the cover off the silver dish.

"Pancakes!" cried the Emperor. "How very nice! Capital!" just as if he didn't have pancakes every day of the year.

Then the fourth and fifth footmen, armed with huge silver forks, began carefully lifting the pancakes from the silver dish, one by one, and laying them on the Emperor's golden plate. Pale yellow, they were, and slightly, ever so slightly brown on top; in fact, just done to a turn; and, of course, they were all as round as round as round.

Out they came, one, two, three, four, five, and each as round and crisp as could be.

And now, as the Emperor reached for the sugar, out came the last pancake. Clang went the silver cover on the silver dish, and the Emperor was just about to dig in, when he stopped.

He stopped and he stared! He stopped and he stared and he gasped!

Then, trembling with fury, he rose slowly to his feet. His face began to turn bright purple, and he tore his white dinner napkin out of his red velvet collar and flung it across the room. Then he opened his mouth and roared.

And what he roared was: "OBLONG!".

Everybody stared in horror, and everybody trembled in fear. Then the five footmen, terrified out of their wits, turned tail and fled through the great bronze doors, which clanged shut behind them.

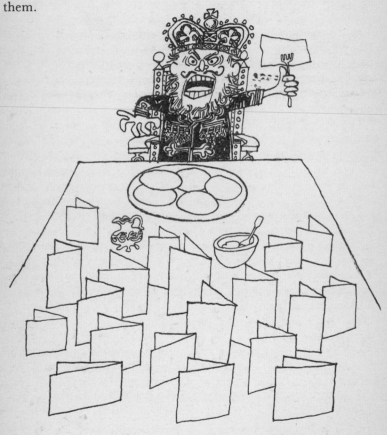

The Court Chamberlain had half a mind to follow them; but then he remembered that before being Court Chamberlain, he had been the bravest corporal in the Emperor's army. So he stood his ground.

"Excellency," said the Court Chamberlain, bowing right down to the ground, and raising his eyebrows at the same time.

"Oblong!" roared the Emperor again; then he stabbed with his fork, plonk right into the middle of the sixth pancake, and raised it high in the air like a flag.

"It's an insult!" he shouted. "This pancake is oblong!"

And so it was; as oblong as oblong as oblong.

The Chamberlain stared at the pancake and the Emperor stared at the Chamberlain.

"Explain!" he roared.

"I . . . I can't, your Excellency," stammered the Chamberlain. "That is, not just at the moment. However, I'll find out about it immediately, immediately, Excellency," and with a somewhat hasty bow he hurried away down the long, marble dining room and out through the bronze double doors.

Left to himself, the Emperor began to feel rather foolish, standing there holding his fork aloft with the oblong pancake dangling from it. Besides, the other five pancakes looked all right. They smelled very nice too, and after all it was his birthday, and he was still hungry.

"Drat the thing!" said the Emperor, and stepping smartly over to the window he hurled the offending pancake as far as he could. Out across the courtyard it flew, and stuck in the top of one of the almond trees, sending a shower of pale pink almond blossoms whirling down on to the marble pavement.

By and by the Emperor finished the five round pancakes, and he was just having an extra piece of toast to make up for the one pancake he hadn't had, when the bronze double doors flew open and the Court Chamberlain hurried in.

He was relieved to find the Emperor looking fairly calm again, and advancing up the long carpet, he bowed low.

"Excellency," he began.

"Well," said the Emperor, rather indistinctly through the toast.

"Excellency, it would appear it was a birthday present."

"A what?" asked the Emperor, a good deal surprised.

"Well, actually, Excellency, and in point of fact," said the Chamberlain, bowing till his forehead touched his shoes, "it was the frying pan."

Then the Emperor began to smile. "I think I see," he said. "The frying pan was a birthday present, and being oblong, it fried an oblong pancake."

The Court Chamberlain straightened up sharply. "Your Excellency's perspicacity is indeed remarkable," he said.

"Oh, I don't know," said the Emperor, modestly, and in fact he didn't, but it sounded complimentary, and he was pleased to have guessed right.

He walked slowly back to his chair, and sat musing a while, twiddling the sugar spoon.

"You know," he said, slowly, "I rather like the idea. An oblong frying pan, eh? Oblong pancakes, what? Yes, I certainly like the idea. After all," he added, "one likes to be a little different, doesn't one?"

The Court Chamberlain was vastly relieved. "Of course, Excellency, exactly," he said. "Oh, yes indeed!"

"Good!" said the Emperor. "Then that's understood, oblong pancakes only in future." And with that he bounced away out of the dining room, as merry as ever, to see to the day's business.

Now that, you might think, was the end of the story. So, indeed, it would have been if this had been an ordinary Emperor; but he wasn't; and he soon made up his mind that everyone in the Empire should share his great discovery. In no time at all the whole population was buying oblong frying pans and frying oblong pancakes; and those who were too poor to buy new ones took hammers or stones or lumps of wood and banged their round frying pans oblong. The Emperor had ordered it, and that was that.

As for the Emperor, he was still as merry as ever, and very pleased with himself for having had such an original idea. For by this time he was quite persuaded he had thought the whole thing out himself. He was still as merry as ever, until one morning in autumn, when the leaves of the almond trees in the courtyard were beginning to turn brown.

On that particular morning the Emperor was just finishing his sixth pancake when an uneasy feeling came over him.

Oblong pancakes, undoubtedly, were the only thing for a man of sense; but something still seemed not quite as it should be. The Emperor pondered, staring at his empty plate; and as he stared he began to smile.

"Of course," he murmured, "why didn't I think of it before? Oblong pancakes need oblong plates. It's common sense." Springing to his feet, he strode across the marble dining room and tugged the bell-pull.

Down in the butler's pantry the Court Chamberlain was just going to start his own oblong pancake when the bell jangled so hard it nearly fell off the wall. Dropping his fork with a clatter, the Chamberlain seized his wand of office and rushed up the marble stairs and through the bronze double doors into the Emperor's dining room. There he bowed low before the Emperor.

"Excellency?" said the Chamberlain, rather out of breath.

"Oblong pancakes need oblong plates," said the Emperor, briefly. "Arrange it."

"Excellency," said the Court Chamberlain, bowing again. And by breakfast-time the next morning, there before the Emperor was a fine golden plate, all new and gleaming, with the imperial arms stamped in the middle. Of course it was oblong.

The Emperor said nothing, but he was pleased all the same. He liked to have his orders promptly obeyed, and besides, one did like to be just a little different.

Of course the Emperor didn't stay different very long, because he soon had every potter and tinsmith in the Empire turning out oblong plates for every man, woman and child in the land. He was so proud of his good idea and besides he was not a selfish man.

But by the end of a week the Emperor was worrying again. He had a tidy mind, and it bothered him to see oblong plates on the table mixed up with cups and saucers which were round. They didn't match. So—you've guessed it—the necessary orders were given, and in no time at all oblong cups and saucers were the rule throughout the country.

By this time the whole idea was beginning to become an obsession. Once started, the Emperor found himself unable to stop, and soon he was ordering something round to be changed to oblong every day.

As for the people, they knew what the Emperor was like when he got hold of an idea, and they soon began to guess what he would change next. Without waiting to be told, they began to throw out everything in their houses which was round, and to have everything oblong instead.

They had oblong saucepans, and oblong spoons and oblong bottles and oblong dishes. They ate oblong pies and oblong tarts and oblong cheeses. They wore oblong hats and they carried oblong umbrellas when it rained. They even bumped about the streets in carriages with oblong wheels. Oh, it was most uncomfortable, but the Emperor was bound to order it sooner or later, and he liked things done so fast, it was best to be prepared.

The Emperor soon learned how the people were so loyal that they tried to anticipate his every wish. But at the same time he couldn't help trying to think of new things to change before they did; and before long he began to order really difficult things like oblong apples and oblong eggs. He was the Emperor, of course, and however difficult it might be, his order must be obeyed. All the farmers and gardeners and all the scientists and professors set to work to see that they were . . . and by the next autumn all the apple trees were loaded with oblong apples, and all the pear trees with oblong pears; and all the hens in the land, poor things, were laying oblong eggs like anything. Even the almonds on the almond trees in the palace courtyard were oblong, and as the Emperor surveyed the scene from his dining room window, he was filled with pride by his own quick thinking and the cleverness of his subjects.

What other monarch, he mused, could have achieved so much in so short a time? He stood there at the window, his hands clasped behind his back, puffing out his chest and surveying the scene with great satisfaction.

Among the oblong almonds the blue and green parakeets flitted and chattered; the fountains splashed gently in their oblong pools; ranged along the far side of the courtyard stood the Emperor's great brass cannons, each with its pile of oblong cannonballs, and over all shone the soft, warm radiance of the autumn sun.

"What a beautiful day," sighed the Emperor contentedly, gazing up at the cloudless blue sky. "What a beautiful, beautiful d . . ."

> *And then he stopped.*
> *He stopped and he stared.*
> *He stopped and he stared and he gasped.*
> *Then he opened his mouth and roared.*
> *And what he roared was: "ROUND!"*

The Court Chamberlain was just putting all the knives and forks and oblong spoons into the silver box marked "Cutlery" when the Emperor roared "ROUND!" and the clatter was dreadful as they flew in all directions over the marble floor.

Pulling himself together, the Court Chamberlain bent low, raising his eyebrows at the same time.

"Excellency?"

"ROUND!" roared the Emperor again. "The sun is round!

Have it changed at once!"

"The sun, Excellency?" stammered the Chamberlain, unable to believe his ears.

"Yes, you fool, the sun!" bellowed the Emperor, fairly dancing with rage. "That ugly, great, yellow, round thing hanging over my lovely oblong empire. It's ruining everything. Change it!"

The Court Chamberlain didn't dare to argue. He knew what the Emperor was like when his mind was made up. So, although he hadn't the slightest idea what he was going to do, "Yes, Excellency," he said, and he bolted out through the bronze double doors.

Once outside, the Chamberlain stopped, pulled out a large red spotted handkerchief and, leaning against a pillar, mopped his brow.

The sun! How in the name of all that was round could anybody make the sun oblong? It was too far away for one thing, and for another it was much too hot.

The Court Chamberlain opened the bronze doors a crack and peeped through. There was the Emperor, still fuming up and down in front of the window, and glaring up at the sun every few seconds, obviously expecting it to turn oblong any moment.

The Chamberlain shut the door, shrugged his shoulders hopelessly, and went off to try.

First he told all the Emperor's woodmen to chop down every tree in the Empire, and then he told all the Emperor's soldiers to build them up into a tall, tall tower, just outside the palace walls.

Every day the tower grew taller, and every day the Chamberlain climbed to the top to see if they were getting anywhere near the sun yet.

By and by there were no more trees left, and the sun seemed as far as ever, so they gave that up.

Then the Chamberlain asked all the Emperor's soldiers if any of them would volunteer to be tied to one of the Emperor's oblong cannonballs and be shot up to the sun with a hammer in his hand. At first none of them would, but at last one of the very bravest said he would try. So they tied him firmly by the middle to an oblong cannonball, and put a heavy hammer in his hand. The Chamberlain told him exactly what to do when he reached the sun, and then they shut their eyes and shot him off.

Up he went like a rocket, but as he was rather fat he didn't go nearly high enough, and he soon came down again and stuck in the top of one of the almond trees in the courtyard; and then he fell out of the tree and splash into one of the oblong fountain pools. A very sorry sight he looked by the time the rest of them hauled him out. Still, they gave him a medal for trying, and the Chamberlain thought again.

He was just working out a method of throwing a stone into the sky without letting go of it, when finally the Emperor lost patience.

He rang all the bells in the palace very loudly, and the Chamberlain and the five footmen and the soldiers, and all the lords and ladies of the court besides, not to mention the people, hurried into the palace courtyard. The Emperor addressed them from the balcony.

"You are the most useless lot of subjects an Emperor ever had," he said crossly. "You don't deserve a progressive monarch like myself. I gave orders three weeks ago for the sun to be made oblong, and look at it—still as round as round as round—horrible!" and the Emperor shuddered.

"We have done our best, Excellency," ventured the Court Chamberlain.

"We've tried and tried and tried," cried all the Emperor's soldiers and the five footmen. All the lords and ladies nodded in agreement, though what they had done goodness only knew.

"Your best is not good enough," said the Emperor, crossly. "You all deserve to be boiled in oil. Instead, however . . ." he paused and surveyed them disdainfully . . . "Instead, however,

37

I shall do the job myself."

"Do you not know," he went on, "that every evening the sun comes down to the edge of the earth? That is the time to deal with it." Then turning to the Court Chamberlain, he said, "Bring out my chariot."

The Chamberlain gave a signal, and the Sergeant-of-Horse led out the chariot, with four black horses dancing and prancing and kicking up the dust, and the Emperor climbed aboard.

They handed him a large packet of dried dates and a parcel of ready cooked pancakes for the journey, and also a pair of blacksmith's tongs and a heavy hammer, which the Emperor stowed under the seat.

Then, pressing his crown firmly on his head, he whipped up the horses, and shot away in a huge cloud of dust.

The people watched the dust cloud grow smaller in the distance until it dwindled out of sight. Then they all went home.

The next morning everyone was up early to see the sunrise. As the first pink glow appeared in the east, all the domes of the palace, and all the roofs in the town were crowded with onlookers. The pink turned to orange, and then to bright yellow, and all the people craned their necks and held their breath.

Then, suddenly, up popped the sun—and all the people groaned. It was still as round as round.

"It must be further than we thought," said the Chamberlain. "No wonder we never reached it with the tower. Still, the Emperor is so determined, he is sure to get there in the end. We shall have to be patient and wait."

So they did. But while they waited, the days grew into weeks and the weeks grew to months, and still the sun came up every morning as round as ever.

Meanwhile, however, some of the people, less patient than the others, began to get tired of bumping about in carriages and carts with oblong wheels. It was really very inconvenient; and so, one by one, they began to change all their oblong wheels back to round ones again. However, they all knew that what they had done was against the Emperor's wishes, so they all pretended not to notice what had happened.

And then, one day, quite suddenly, very much to everyone's surprise, and his own as well, the Emperor came back.

"Well I never!" said the Emperor, climbing stiffly out of his chariot. Everybody stared, and said "Well I never!" too.

"I must have taken a wrong turning somewhere," went on the Emperor, feeling rather foolish. "How very, very annoying!"

So the Chamberlain arranged for the Emperor to have a wash and brush up and a little something to keep out the cold; and they stocked up the chariot again with food for the journey. Then, amid the cheers of all the people, the Emperor drove away to the west once more, and vanished over the horizon.

Again the days passed, and the weeks as well, but still the sun was as round as round; and not only the sun. I am afraid the people started to change other things besides the carriage wheels. It was a great strain on all the hens to keep laying oblong eggs, so they were allowed to go back to laying round ones; and of course that meant changing back all the egg cups as well. They were beginning to change the egg spoons too, when the Emperor suddenly came back again.

"Oh, bother!" said the Emperor, jumping crossly from his chariot. "I seem to have gone wrong again." But he was very determined, as you know by now, and he wouldn't give up. However, just to see what happened, this time he pointed his chariot the other way, and galloped rapidly away towards the east. Immediately everyone went back to changing the spoons, and because the gardeners had forgotten to use the special fertilizer, all the fruit trees began to produce ordinary, round apples and oranges and pears and almonds once more.

And so it went on for a long while. The sun stayed as round as round, and gradually everything in the Empire which had once been oblong was changed to being round too. Every now and then the Emperor would suddenly arrive back again, and say "Oh, bother!" and gallop off in a new direction.

But as time passed it became clear that no matter in which direction he galloped, he always came back again to where he had started from. No one could understand it.

Then one day in spring, when the almond trees in the palace courtyard were bursting into blossom, the Emperor came back for the umpteenth time; but this time he didn't say, "Oh, bother!" Instead he came galloping up as merry as could be, and bounced out of his chariot and up the marble staircase into the palace.

Then he rang all the bells, and summoned the people into the courtyard.

Soon they were assembled, but they held their hats behind their backs, because, of course, they were all round, and they didn't want the Emperor to see. The Sergeant of the Guard had sentries stationed in front of the cannons, so as to hide the piles of round cannon balls from the Emperor.

The Emperor, looking very pleased with himself, stepped out on to the balcony, and addressed them.

"My people," he began, "you have been very patient. I have been away a long time, and you have remained loyal and obedient subjects in every way. I am very pleased with you all."

At this the people cheered, but they felt a little nervous, and no one more so than the Chamberlain. He could not help remembering all the things which had been changed from oblong to round against the Emperor's wishes.

But the Emperor was speaking again.

"My people," he said, "I have failed to reach the sun; but . . ." and he began to smile broadly, and puffed out his chest till all his decorations rattled and the buttons nearly flew off his waistcoat. "It no longer matters. Changing the sun is a very minor matter, after all, compared with the remarkable discovery I have made. My people," said the Emperor, proudly, "my dear people, your Emperor has established by personal experiment, and beyond all reasonable doubt, a new and amazing scientific fact. The world, in short . . . .

THE WORLD IS ROUND!"

You should have heard the cheering. The people cheered, and the soldiers cheered, the footmen cheered, the lords and ladies cheered; and none cheered louder than the Chamberlain.

The Emperor bowed and smiled, and smiled and bowed, and then he held his hand up again.

"The world is round, my people, as round as round as round. And very nice, too. So now, in consequence, it is my wish that everything in the Empire should be round as well— to match."

The Court Chamberlain stepped forward and bowed as low as low: "Your Excellency," he said, "may it please your Excellency, it is already done."

The Emperor was so pleased at this that he danced a little jig, clapping his hands and crying "Capital, capital, capital!"

Then the Emperor turned and entered the marble dining room, followed by the Chamberlain and the five footmen.

"Now," said the Emperor, rubbing his hands, "what about breakfast?"

"May I suggest pancakes, your Excellency?" ventured the Court Chamberlain with a smile.

"Excellent!" said the Emperor. "Nothing could be nicer."

"Would your Excellency prefer them round or— or—oblong?" inquired the Chamberlain, bowing as low as low.

The Emperor thought for a moment, rubbing his chin, and then his eyes twinkled, and he said: "Oblong, please. I shall continue to have my pancakes oblong. After all the frying pan was a birthday present, and I wouldn't like to hurt anyone's feelings. And besides," finished the Emperor, settling comfortably in his chair, "besides, one does like to be a little different, after all!"

Big Claus and Little Claus

Once upon a time there were two men who lived in the same town and had the same name—both were called Claus. But one of them had four horses and the other only one. So to tell one from the other, they called the one who owned four horses Big Claus and the one who owned only one horse Little Claus. And now let's find out how these two got on together, for it really is quite a story.

For six days of the week Little Claus had to do the ploughing for Big Claus and lend him his one horse. In return Big Claus would help Little Claus with his four horses—but only once a week, on Sundays. And how Little Claus would crack down his whip on all five horses on Sundays, when the horses were his. The sun would shine so bright, the bells in the church would peal out loud and clear and people would walk by in their very best clothes with their hymn-books under their arms, on their way to hear the vicar preach his sermon, and they would see Little Claus ploughing away with five horses. And he would feel so happy that he would bring down his whip with a resounding thwack! and cry: "Gee-up there, all my horses."

"Don't SAY that," warned Big Claus. "Only one of them is yours."

But as soon as anyone passed by again on the way to church, Little Claus would forget about this and he would cry out: "Gee-up there, all my horses."

"Now stop that at once, if you please," warned Big Claus

42

again. "If you say it just once more, I'll crack your horse over the head and kill him dead; and that'll be the end of him."

"I won't say it again, I promise," said Little Claus. But when the people walked by and nodded Good-day he would feel so happy and so grand to have five horses that he would crack his whip and cry out, "Gee-up there, all my horses!"

"I'll teach you to gee-up your horses," said Big Claus and, taking a mallet, he brought down such a mighty crack on the head of Little Claus's only horse that it fell down dead on the spot.

"Oh dear," wailed Little Claus. "Now I haven't got a horse at all." And he started to cry. But he didn't cry for very long. He stripped the hide off his dead horse and then left the hide to dry in the wind. Then he put it into a bag, threw the bag over his shoulders and set off to sell the horse-hide in the nearest town.

It was a very long way, through a great dark wood, and all of a sudden there was a terrible storm. Little Claus was quite lost and wandered all over the place until at last he found himself outside a large farmhouse. The shutters were up, for it was already nightfall, but he could see a small light shining over the top of them.

"I expect they will put me up for the night," thought Little Claus and he went and knocked at the door.

The farmer's wife opened it. When she heard what he wanted she said: "You can't come in here. My husband is away and I don't take strangers in." And with that she shut the door in his face.

Little Claus looked round. There was a haystack close by and between that and the farmhouse there was a shed with a flat thatched roof.

"I can sleep up there," thought Little Claus, looking up at the roof. "It should make a fine bed. I don't imagine that stork will fly down and peck my legs" (for, standing on the roof, was a real stork which had built its nest there).

So up he climbed on to the shed and lay down and wriggled about till he was nice and comfortable. The shutters on the farmhouse windows did not quite fit at the top, so he was able to look over them, right inside, and see what was going on.

He could see a big table spread with roast meat and red wine and some very tasty-looking fish. The farmer's wife and the village schoolmaster were sitting there and she was filling up his glass and he was helping himself to the fish, to which he seemed to be very partial.

"Wouldn't I just like to have some of that!" thought Little Claus, sticking his head as close to the window as he could. "Goodness me, what a splendid cake! What a feast they're having!"

Just then he heard the sound of horses' hooves along the high road. They were coming towards the house: it was the woman's husband coming home. He was a most worthy man but he had one rather strange weakness—he couldn't stand the sight of village schoolmasters. The mere mention of one would send him mad with rage, which was why the schoolmaster was visiting the farmer's wife when her husband was away and why she was now offering him her tastiest dishes. So now, when they heard her husband coming, they both got very frightened and the woman told the schoolmaster to hide in a large empty chest in the corner. Which he did at once, and the woman quickly put away all the delicious food and wine in her oven, for if her husband had seen them he would certainly have asked what it all meant.

"Oh what a shame," sighed Little Claus from his thatched bed, when he saw all the appetising food disappear into the oven.

"Who is that up there?" called the farmer, looking up at Little Claus. "Why are you lying there? Come indoors with me."

Little Claus then told him about the storm and how he had lost his way and asked the good farmer if he could put him up for the night.

"Most certainly," said the farmer, "but first let's have a bite of supper."

The farmer's wife had now become all friendly and welcomed Little Claus when she saw him at the door with her husband. She spread the cloth on the long table and served them a large bowl of porridge. The farmer ate heartily enough but Little Claus could not take his mind off the delicious roast meat and fish and the wine and the cake which he knew were in the oven. Under the table at his feet was the bag with the horse-hide. He trod on the bag and the dry hide gave out a loud squeak.

"Hush!" said Little Claus pretending to listen to something, and he trod on it again, making it squeak even louder.

"Hullo," said the farmer, "what's that you've got under there?"

"Oh, that's my wizard. I keep him in my bag," replied Little Claus. "He says we are not to eat the porridge for he's conjured the whole oven full of roast meat, fish, cake and red wine."

"What! What!" exclaimed the farmer, and stretching over to the oven, he opened it and saw all the delicious food his wife had hidden away there but which he believed the wizard had conjured up for him.

His wife, not daring to say a word, placed all the food on the table at once and they helped themselves freely. When they had eaten and drunk to their hearts' content, the farmer became quite jolly and asked: "What else can your wizard do? Can he call up the Devil, I wonder? I'd like to see him do that."

"Oh yes," said Little Claus, "my wizard will do anything I ask—won't you?" and he trod on his bag again. "Did you hear him say 'yes'? But the Devil is not very pretty to look at and I shouldn't bother to see him if I were you."

"Oh I'm not afraid," said the farmer. "What does he really look like?"

"Well, as far as I know, he may well show himself looking like a village schoolmaster."

"Ugh!" grunted the farmer with a start, "I can't stand .the

sight of village schoolmasters. But, no matter, as long as I know it's the Devil I shan't mind. I'm quite brave—but don't let him come too near me, mind."

"I'll ask my wizard then," said Little Claus, and he trod on his bag and bent down to listen.

"What does he say?" asked the farmer.

"He says: 'Go over to that chest in the corner and you'll find the Devil crouching inside.' But hold the lid firm so that he doesn't slip out."

The farmer went over to the chest, lifted the lid and peeped inside.

"Ugh!" he shrieked and shrank back. "He looks the very image of our village schoolmaster. What a horrid sight!" And then they drank some more wine to get over the shock, and in fact they went on drinking all through the night.

"You know, you'll have to sell me that wizard of yours," said the farmer. "I'll pay you as much as you like—a whole bushel of money, just say the word."

"Oh no!" said Little Claus. "Just think of all the things he can do for me."

"Oh please," begged the farmer, "I simply must have that wizard. I'd give anything in the world for him."

"Oh very well then," said Little Claus. "As you've been kind enough to give me a night's lodging, you can have my wizard for a bushel of money, but I insist on a full measure."

"Of course," said the farmer, "but see that that chest is taken away. I won't have it in my home one moment longer. He may still be inside," he added with a shudder.

Little Claus gave the farmer his bag with the dry horse-hide and in return received a whole bushel of money, full measure. The farmer also gave him a wheelbarrow to wheel away the money and the chest.

"Good-bye," said Little Claus and off he went, wheeling the barrow with the bushel of money and the chest (with the village schoolmaster inside).

He reached the other side of the forest where there was a deep, swiftly-flowing river. A fine new bridge had been built across it and when he was about half-way across, Little Claus said, loud enough for the schoolmaster to hear: "Now what am I to do with this silly old chest? It's no use to me. I'd better heave it into the river and get rid of it." And he took hold of one end and lifted it up a bit.

"No, stop!" cried the village schoolmaster from inside the chest. "Let me out! Let me out!"

"Ugh!" cried Little Claus, pretending to be scared. "He's still there! I'd better drop it straight into the river and drown him before he gets out."

"Oh no!" pleaded the village schoolmaster. "Let me out and I'll give you a whole bushel of money."

"Well, that's different," said Little Claus, opening the chest and letting out the village schoolmaster. Little Claus pushed the chest into the river and the schoolmaster ran home and came back to give Little Claus another whole bushel of money.

"I seem to have got a pretty good price for that horse of mine," he said to himself when he got home and counted out his two bushels of money. "Big Claus will be none too pleased when he finds out how rich I've grown from my one horse."

Soon after this he sent a boy over to Big Claus to borrow a bushel measure. "What on earth can he want that for?" won-

dered Big Claus, and he stuck a bit of tar at the botom of it so
that whatever Little Claus was measuring would stick to it. And
indeed that is just what did happen. For when the measure was
returned to Big Claus there were two gleaming silver florins
sticking to it.

"What does this mean?" said Big Claus and he dashed
straight off to Little Claus and asked, "Where have you got all
this money from?"

"Oh that's from the horse-hide which I sold yesterday."

"And a handsome price you must have got for it," said Big
Claus. And he hurried back home, took an axe and struck all
his four horses down dead. Then he stripped their skins off and
drove off to town with them.

"Skins, horses' skins! Who'll buy my skins?" he shouted as
he went through the streets. All the tanners and shoemakers
came out and asked what price he was asking.

"A bushel of money per piece," he replied.

"A bushel of money!" they all cried in amazement. "Are you
mad? D'you think we are fools?" And they took their straps
and leather aprons and began to beat him and thrash him until
he was chased right out of town. When he got back home that
night he was very angry. "Little Claus will pay for this," he
kept muttering. "He'll pay with his life for this. I'll kill him."

Just about this time Little Claus's grandmother died. It's true
she hadn't been very kind to him (at times she had even been
quite nasty), but he felt very sorry all the same and so he took
the dead lady over into his own warm bed to see if he could
bring her back to life again. He left her there all night and he
went and slept in a chair in a corner of the room.

In the middle of the night the door opened and in crept Big
Claus with his axe. He made straight for the bed and hit the
dead grandmother on the head, thinking it was Little Claus.

"Well, that's finished him," he muttered to himself, "he won't
make a fool of me again." And he went off home.

"Well, well," said Little Claus. "What a nasty, wicked man.

48

He meant that blow with the axe for me. It's a good thing old grandmother was dead already or he'd have well and truly done the job himself."

He then dressed his granny in her Sunday best, borrowed a horse and cart from a neighbour and propped the old lady up on the back seat so that she wouldn't slump out if he drove too fast. Then he started out through the forest. He reached an inn just about sunrise and went inside to have a bite of something to eat.

Mine host the innkeeper was a very rich and very pleasant man on the whole, but there were times when he could get very peppery and lose his temper completely.

"Good morning," he said to Little Claus. "I see you're out early today, and in your best clothes too."

"Yes," said Little Claus, "I'm off to town with my grandmother. She's sitting out there in the back seat of the cart. She won't come in, so would you kindly take her out a glass of mead. And speak up loud, won't you, as her hearing is not all that good."

The innkeeper went out to her. "Here's a glass of mead from your grandson, madam," he said.

The dead lady said never a word and sat quite still.

49

"Can't you hear?" shouted the innkeeper at the top of his voice. "Here's a glass of mead from your grandson!" He shouted the same thing again and again and as she didn't stir he flew into a rage, completely lost his temper and threw the glass right in the dead lady's face. The mead ran down all over her cheeks and nose and she slumped over the side of the cart—for Little Claus had only propped her up and not tied her fast.

"Now look what you've done!" shouted Little Claus, rushing out of the inn. "You've killed my poor grandmother. Just look at that great cut in her forehead."

"Oh what a misfortune!" cried the innkeeper, wringing his hands. "It's all because of my hot temper. Dear Little Claus! I'll give you a whole bushel of money and have her buried as though she were my own grandmother. Only don't tell anyone, of course, or they'll cut my head off and that wouldn't be at all nice."

And so Little Claus got another bushel of money and the innkeeper buried the old granny as if she had been his own.

Then Little Claus went back home and sent a boy over to Big Claus to ask if he could borrow a bushel measure.

"My goodness, what can that mean?" wondered Big Claus. "I killed him, didn't I? I'd better go and see for myself." So off he went to Little Claus with the bushel measure.

When he saw all the money he gaped with surprise. "Where did all this come from?" he asked.

"You didn't kill me," said Little Claus. "It was my grandmother you killed with your axe. And I've sold her for a bushel of money."

"My goodness, that's a pretty good price you've got for her," said Big Claus, and he hurried straight home and killed his grandmother with his axe. Then he put her in a cart and drove to the chemist's and asked him if he wanted to buy a dead body.

"Whose?" asked the chemist. "And where did you get it?"

"It's my grandmother," replied Big Claus. "I've killed her and I'm asking a bushel of money for her."

"Heavens above!" cried the chemist. "What next, I wonder! You must be raving mad. If you go about saying things like that, you'll lose your own head. You're a very wicked man and you deserve to be punished!"

Big Claus got so frightened at this that he rushed out of the shop, jumped into his cart and galloped his horse straight back to his house. The chemist really thought he must have gone mad—and so did everyone else—and they let him drive wherever he wanted to.

Big Claus really was mad— with rage. "You'll pay for this, Little Claus," he kept saying. "You'll most surely pay for this." And as soon as he was back home, he took the biggest sack he could find and went over to Little Claus and said: "So you've fooled me again, have you? First, you made me kill my horses and now my grandmother. But you are never going to fool me again!" So saying, he seized Little Claus by the scruff of the neck, put him into the sack and slung the sack over his shoulder. "And now, Little Claus, I'm going to drown you," he said.

Little Claus was no lightweight and Big Claus had a long way to go before he got to the river. Along the road they passed a church where they could hear people singing hymns to the accompaniment of a beautiful organ. "It would be rather nice if I went in and sang a hymn before I go any further," thought Big Claus, and so he put down his heavy burden and went into the church. "Oh dear! Oh dear!" Little Claus kept saying as he twisted and turned in the sack; but he couldn't untie the cord. At that moment an old cattle drover was passing, with a big stick in his hand and driving a herd of cows and bullocks. One or two of them stumbled against the sack and knocked it over.

"Oh dear!" sighed Little Claus. "I'm so very young and I'm going to heaven already."

"And I'm so very old," said the drover, "and I can't get there yet!"

"Open the sack," cried Little Claus. "Change places with me

51

and you'll go to heaven straight away!"

"Gladly will I do that," said the old drover, and he undid the sack and out jumped Little Claus.

"You *will* look after my cattle," said the drover, getting into the sack.

"To be sure, I will," said Little Claus, and he tied up the sack and then went off with the cows and bullocks.

Soon Big Claus came out of church and flung the sack over his shoulder, thinking how light it had become—the old drover was less than half the weight of Little Claus. "He's grown light as a feather," he muttered to himself. "It must be the effect of that nice hymn I have sung." Then he made for the river which was deep and wide, and threw in the sack with the old drover inside.

"Take that, Little Claus," he shouted, "you'll not fool me any more."

He then set off home, but at the crossroads whom should he meet but Little Claus himself, driving his herd of cows and bullocks.

"What does this mean?" asked Big Claus. "Didn't I just throw you into the river?"

"Yes, you did," said Little Claus.

"Then where have you got all this cattle from?"

"It's sea-cattle," said Little Claus. "I'm very grateful to you for throwing me in, but let me tell you the whole story. I was really terribly frightened when I was tied up inside that sack, and how the wind did howl when you threw me down from the bridge. I went straight to the bottom, of course, only I didn't get hurt because I fell on to the softest of soft grass that grows on the river bed. And then the sack opened and the loveliest of lovely girls in a snow-white dress, with a white garland round her hair, came and took me by the hand and said: 'Is that you, Little Claus? Here's some cattle for you, and a mile further along there's another herd for you.' I then saw that the river was a wide sea-road for the sea-people. They were walking along down at the bottom, making their way up to the country where the sea ends. I can't tell you how pleasant it was down there, with flowers and green grass, and fishes darting past like birds in the air. And cattle, too, walking along the dikes and ditches."

"Then whatever made you come up again so soon?" asked Big Claus. "I would have stayed down much longer, as it seems so very nice down there."

"Well," replied Little Claus. "Listen to me, this will just show you how clever I am. You remember I told you the sea-girl said there was another herd of cattle waiting for me. Well, I know the river winds and bends all over the place so I have decided to make a short cut by coming up on land and then diving down into the river again. I'll save almost half a mile like that, and I'll get the rest of my cattle all the quicker."

"I must say, you *are* a lucky man," said Big Claus. "Do you think I could get some sea-cattle if I went down to the bottom of the river?"

"I don't see why you shouldn't," replied Little Claus. "But don't ask me to carry you to the river in a sack, you are far too heavy for me. If you care to walk there and then get into the sack, I'll throw you in with the greatest of pleasure."

"Thank you very much," said Big Claus, "but if I don't get any sea-cattle when I get down there, you can look out! I'll give you the thrashing of your life!"

"Oh please don't be too hard on me," said Little Claus, and off they went across to the river. When the cattle saw the water they ran towards it as fast as ever they could, for they were very thirsty.

"You can see how eager they are to get to the bottom again," said Little Claus.

"Yes, yes," said Big Claus impatiently. "I can see that, but you've got to help me to get in first or else you'll get that thrashing I promised you."

"Very well," said Little Claus, helping Big Claus to get into the sack. "And put a stone in it in case I don't sink," added Big

Claus as his head disappeared inside the sack.

"You'll sink all right," said Little Claus. And putting in a large stone, he tied the cord tight and pushed the sack into the flowing water.

"I'm very much afraid he won't get that cattle," said Little Claus, and he drove off back home with what he had got.

The Wishing-skin

Once upon a time there was a woodcutter whose name was Rudolf. He was very poor, and he lived with his wife in a little hut made of split logs, in the middle of a deep forest.

The forest was so thick that people scarcely ever passed Rudolf's hut. But the woodcutter wasn't lonely. When he was at home he sat by the fire, talking to his wife; and when he was in the woods, he made friends with the birds and the animals. The furry beasts and the little feathered folk used to watch him out of their bright eyes and come quite close to his feet without being afraid. Then Rudolf would look at them and say: "Good morning, little comrades! I'd rather have friends like you than all the riches in the world."

One day the king came hunting in the woods, looking for wild deer. Princes and princesses came with him, and lords and ladies too. They came once. They came twice. They came three times. And they liked it so much that after that they came nearly every day.

Their clothes were of velvet edged with fur. They rode fine horses with little silver bells round their necks, and they had servants dressed in green and gold who brought baskets of food for them to eat when they were hungry, and flasks of sparkling wine to drink when they were thirsty.

Sometimes they stopped at Rudolf's little hut and peeped in and laughed, saying: "See the funny old table with no fine

55

linen! Look, he hasn't any chairs! How quaint! How old-fashioned!" and they would sit on Rudolf's three-legged stools and say: "Ooh, how hard! He must wear out his breeches without a velvet cushion." And when they saw the darns and patches in Rudolf's breeches, they laughed and said: "Ha! Ha! We were right." When Rudolf heard this he was ashamed of his poor hut and his ugly, darned breeches, and little by little he began to grow discontented.

He began to wonder why he should be poor and they rich, and he went about his work with such a long face that the birds were afraid of him, and he heaved such deep, grumbling sighs that all the little beasts scuttled into the woods in a fright—at least, all save the rabbit.

The rabbit sat back on his haunches, flopped his ears and wobbled his nose. "Why, what's the matter with you, Rudolf?"

"Nothing," said Rudolf, grumpily. "I wish I were rich. That's all."

"Pah," said the rabbit. "What's the good of wishing without the wishing-skin? Spare your breath, Rudolf."

Rudolf straightened his back and put down his hatchet. "Eh?" said he. "Wishing-skin, did you say? And what may that be, Bunny?"

The rabbit whisked round with a flicker of his white tail. "Half a minute," he said, "I'll show you," and he skipped behind a bush, returning almost at once with a thin, cobwebby skin. "There, that's the wishing-skin. But don't tell anyone you've seen it. It belongs to the fairies, and they always hide it. They're afraid of its being stolen. You see it's very valuable. It's made of wishes."

Rudolf looked at the rabbit out of the corner of his eye, cunningly. "Bunny," said he, "suppose I try it on? I'd like to know what it's like to wear a wishing-skin."

The rabbit looked doubtful.

"Well," said he, after a pause, "I don't know whether I ought to let you do that. It's not mine, and, you know, if you were to wish by accident after you had put it on, the fairies would know and I should get into trouble. You see, whenever you wish, the skin gets a little smaller, because one wish is gone. If you're wearing the wishing-skin all your wishes come true."

Rudolf's hands began to shake, so he put them behind his back. "Don't be so silly, Bunny," said he. "As if I should get you into trouble. Let me try it on. Come on! See, I've taken off my coat."

He put his coat on the ground and then—well, then, I'm afraid, he did rather a mean thing. He clapped his hands suddenly so that the rabbit jumped backwards in a fright and before the startled little creature could do anything, Rudolf had put on the wishing-skin and was grinning from ear to ear.

"Ha, ha, ha!" he laughed. "I wish it would stick to me and become a part of me."

"Oh! Oh!" cried the rabbit. "Give it back! What will the fairies say? You've made it smaller already." He stamped with his hind legs on the ground and his eyes looked as if they were going to pop out of his head. "Do you hear me? Give it back!"

"How can I?" grinned Rudolf. "It's a part of me, stupid!"

"Oh!" wailed the rabbit. "Give it back!" And he cried so bitterly that Rudolf was a little ashamed, and somehow, because he was ashamed he grew angry.

"Will you be quiet?" said he. "I wish you were at the other end of the earth, I do, with your 'Give it backs'. I—" He stopped and rubbed his eyes. The rabbit had disappeared.

"Why! What?" began Rudolf. Then he remembered. He had wished the rabbit at the other end of the earth, and the wishing-skin had sent it there.

"Hurrah!" shouted Rudolf, capering about. "Hurrah! Now I can get whatever I want." And he picked up his coat and ran back to his hut as hard as he could. When he reached the door, he thought for a few minutes, then he walked in and sat down by the fire. "Wife," said he, "have you got a good supper—chicken and sauce and sausages?"

The Wishing-skin

His wife stared at him, half afraid. "Have you gone mad, Rudolf?" she asked. "Chicken, sauce, sausages! Here's your good bread and honey."

"Pooh!" said Rudolf. "I wish for chicken, sauce and sausages! I wish for wine! I wish for a nice table spread with fine linen, with silver spoons and golden plates! I wish for chairs and velvet cushions!"

"Stop! Stop!" cried his wife, falling into one of the new chairs, for the wishes were coming true every minute. "How?— What?—Why?—"

"The wishing-skin, my dear," said her husband. And then he told her all about it.

You should have seen that woman's face. It grew quite red, and the eyes goggled! You ought to have heard what she said. But if you had heard that, well, you wouldn't have heard very much, because she was almost too astonished to speak. But when she recovered from her amazement, she wouldn't give her husband any peace. She simply made him wish all night. It was "Wish for this!" "Wish for that!" "Now wish for fine clothes," and they found themselves beautifully dressed. "Now wish for six bags of gold," and on the table there were six bags of golden coins. "Now wish for a fine house, and a garden full of flowers and lots and lots of servants." And instead of the little wooden hut at the edge of the forest, a fine house appeared with a garden full of flowers and servants everywhere! Cooks in the kitchen, butlers in the pantry, maids in the bedrooms, and footmen with powdered wigs and silk stockings standing on each side of every stair (and there were three flights of stairs).

But you know, it was all very well to have such riches—but to tell you the truth, a dreadful thing was happening! Rudolf's wife was so busy making him wish, that she didn't notice that her husband was shrinking. Yes! Rudolf was getting smaller.

You see how it was happening, don't you?

Of course you do! Don't you remember? Rudolf had wished the skin to become a part of himself. Each time he wished it

became smaller, so of course he became smaller too.

Poor old Rudolf! He didn't like it at all. He was afraid to wish himself bigger, because then he might burst out of the wishing-skin and it would be of no more use. The difficulty was that his wife wouldn't be satisfied. She went on making him wish, until at last she wished that he was a king and she was a queen in the most beautiful palace in the land.

But, oh dear, it wasn't very nice for Rudolf. You see, by this time he had become so small that he had to have his meals, not at the table, but on the table. He had a special little throne, like a doll's chair, and a special little table made by the carpenter. They were put on the big table in the banqueting hall and there the little king had his meals. This was rather undignified for a king, don't you think? I am afraid everybody who came into the banqueting hall thought so too, even the servants. They couldn't help being amused when they had to hand the dishes and pour out tiny glasses of wine for the queer little object sitting on the table. And all the grand lords and ladies who came to visit the new king and queen felt exactly the same. They did their best to be polite, but the little king sitting on the table seemed such a joke that they couldn't help playing with him as though he were a toy. And that was dreadful, because Rudolf still had the feelings of a grown-up man, although he was so small.

After a time something happened which was worse still. Rudolf's wife began to despise him. She was offended and angry when people laughed at him because she thought they were laughing at her for having such a silly little husband. She tried to prevent Rudolf from coming into the banqueting hall and hurried him out of the way whenever she was expecting an important visitor. At last, she hid him from sight. She built him a tiny doll's house in the garden and never went to see him except when she wanted him to wish for something.

You can imagine how lonely he was, can't you? Poor little king! He used to get up in the morning and put on his crown and look out of the window, wondering how much smaller he was going to get and whether he would soon disappear altogether.

Then, one day when he was looking out of the window, a woodcutter chanced to walk by. He had a hatchet in his hand and a load of wood on his shoulders, and he walked along the path past the doll's house whistling a tune and looking ever so happy.

Rudolf saw him and sighed deeply. "Oh!" he cried, "how I

envy that happy man. I wish I could forget all this and be a woodcutter with my wife and cottage again!"

A cold wind suddenly blew in his face. He looked up and— well, if you had peeped into the forest at that moment you would have seen Rudolf picking up a bundle of faggots—and at his feet a little brown rabbit. And the rabbit—yes, I think the rabbit would have been a little out of breath.

The Fox and the Stork

◆

One day a fox thought he would have a bit of a joke at the stork's expense.

He invited him to dinner and served up the soup in very shallow dishes. The fox lapped up his portion very easily but the poor old stork, with his long, thin beak, was quite helpless and unable to manage a single beakful. The fox pretended to be most upset and said he was sorry his guest did not seem to like the soup. The stork did not say anything to this but thanked the fox for his hospitality and left as hungry as when he had arrived.

Shortly after, the stork invited the fox to a return meal. The fox accepted the invitation very readily. However, when the meal was served up he was disgusted to find that the food was in very tall, very narrow dishes, and he hardly managed to get his lips beyond the rim. He had to sit there hungry, watching the stork thrusting his long slender beak right down to the bottom of the dish and gathering up every single morsel of food.

"I am very sorry my food is not to your taste," said the stork, pretending to be most concerned.

The fox said nothing but left with a very sour face, muttering to himself, "It serves me right, I suppose. The stork has certainly paid me back in my own coin."

Clever Stan and the Stupid Dragon

◆

Why was Stan Bolovan an unhappy man? He had a comfortable house, two healthy cows and a garden with lots of fruit trees. Well, it was his wife. She was *always* crying. And I mean always. In the morning, after dinner, after supper and even when it was time to go to bed. In other respects she was quite a good sort, really.

You might have thought that she would have told Stan (who was a good husband) *why* she was always crying. But no. She would not tell him. "Leave me alone," she would say. "You wouldn't understand, even if I did tell you." But he kept on pestering her day after day, week after week, month after month, until at last, one fine day, she *did* tell him. "I keep crying," she said tearfully, "because we haven't got any children." When Stan heard this, he too became all sad and miserable, and so the Bolovan household wasn't a very cheerful place, I can tell you.

Stan decided to consult a magician. The magician gazed long into the crystal globe and said not a word. Stan waited and waited until at last he became impatient.

"Come on," he said, "I want your help. Say something."

The magician looked up at him. "Are you quite certain you want children?" he asked. "They can be a great burden, you know."

"Yes, I know," said Stan, "but what a happy burden; it's the kind of burden my wife and I are dying to have."

"Very well then," said the magician, "you shall have your wish."

Stan left with a light heart and started back on his journey home (for he had come a long way to see the magician). He was longing to tell his wife the good news. "How marvellous!" he thought. "There'll be no more crying from now on, not from my wife at any rate."

Imagine his surprise, when he reached the door of his house, at hearing the sound of children's voices laughing and chattering, and little feet pattering all over the place. He went round into the garden and a wonderful sight met his eyes. There were dozens and dozens of children of all shapes and sizes, fat ones and thin ones, tall ones and short ones, children with fair hair and blue eyes and children with dark hair and brown eyes, children with curls and children with straight hair, quiet children and noisy children, cheeky children and shy children

Clever Stan and the Stupid Dragon

—in fact every imaginable variety.

"Good heavens," said Stan Bolovan to his wife, "there must be at least a hundred children here!"

"And every one of them welcome," smiled his wife.

"But how on earth are we going to clothe and feed them all?" asked Stan, perplexed. But his wife only went on smiling. He soon found that she had given all the milk and all the fruit to the children and there wasn't a morsel of food left in the house.

So Stan Bolovan set out to find food and clothing for his children.

After walking for nearly a whole day, he espied a shepherd who was herding his many sheep and lambs in a field.

"I know it's the wrong thing to do," thought poor Stan Bolovan, "but if I wait till it's dark I might be able to get a lamb or two and feed my hungry children with some juicy meat." He hid behind a stout oak tree and waited for night to fall. Suddenly, round about midnight, he heard a great whirring, rushing sound in the skies and lo and behold! he looked up and saw a dragon swooping from a great height straight down among the sheep. It picked up a lamb in each of its four paws and flew up again.

The poor old shepherd was running about all over the place, trying to keep his fear-crazed flock together and Stan Bolovan decided to help him. At last, when they had restored some sort of order, they sat down against a tree to rest.

"You know," sighed the shepherd, "this happens every single night. If things go on like this I soon won't have a sheep to my name." He thanked Stan for his help and offered him some bread and cheese. This made Stan feel very much better.

"What will you give me," he asked, "if I rid you of that dragon?"

"I'll give you as much food and drink as you like, as well as three rams, three sheep and three lambs."

"That's a bargain," said Stan, not having the slightest idea how he was going to conquer the dragon.

He spent the next day helping the shepherd and thinking about his hungry brood of children. As night drew on, a great dread seized him and it was all he could do to stop himself shaking and shivering with fear.

At midnight the air was suddenly filled with the fierce whirring and rushing sound and the fearsome dragon, his scales gleaming in the moonlight, came swooping down amid the sheep.

Stan Bolovan, feeling quite crazily bold, stood up and bawled: "Stop! Stop at once!"

The beast, quite taken aback, sank slowly to the ground.

"And may I inquire to whom I 'ave the *h*onour of speakin'?" he said somewhat breathlessly.

"I am Stan Bolovan. Stan Bolovan the Mighty, eater-up of rocks and gobbler of mountains. One move from you towards those sheep and I'll gobble *you* up."

The dragon, for want of anything better to say, muttered grimly: "You'll have to fight me first."

"Please don't invite me to fight you," said Stan Bolovan. "I'd kill you with one breath and your corpse would be nice filling for my sandwiches."

The dragon was a terrible coward at heart.

"Well, I've got to be goin' now," he said. "I'll bid ye goodnight."

"Steady on," said Stan, "we've got an account to settle first, haven't we now?"

"What? What? What account?" asked the dragon nervously.

"Those sheep you've been stealing every night," said Stan Bolovan. "They are my sheep, you know. That man over there is a shepherd who works for me. You'd better settle up here and now, or there'll be trouble."

The dragon, of course, had no money on him and he had no wish to be made into filling for Stan's sandwiches, so he said: "My old mother has stacks and stacks of money. Come and stay with us just for three or four days and help her about the house. If she likes you, she'll give you ten sacks of gold every day."

"Very well," said Stan Bolovan, getting bolder and bolder every minute. "Lead me to her." He thought what a lot of food and clothing ten sacks of gold would buy for his hundred children. "I'll face the old dragoness even if it kills me."

So off they went to the dragon's residence and found the dragon's mother waiting outside the door. Her first words were not terribly encouraging. "What!" she shrieked, her scales standing up in fury. "No sheep!"

"Sh!" said the dragon soothingly. "I've brought you a visitor." And to Stan he whispered: "Don't worry, I'll go and explain."

Stan waited outside. He could hear the dragon's quite audible whispers: "This chap's a terror; he devours rocks and mountains and uses dead dragons as filling for his sandwiches."

"Leave him to me," said the mother dragon, not even bothering to lower her voice, "*I'll* see to him."

They called Stan in and showed him to a great bed where he was to sleep for the night. But he hardly had a wink of sleep. He kept having nightmares about the mother dragon with her bulging green eyes and ugly black scales.

Next morning she said to Stan: "Let me see whether you are really stronger than my son." And she picked up an enormous metal barrel bound round with iron hoops. The dragon took hold of it and hurled it with all his might and Stan heard it crash into the ground at what seemed like miles and miles away. He and the dragon walked after it and found it buried in the earth of a mountain-side about three miles off.

"Your turn," said the dragon. Stan Bolovan, playing for time, looked down at it and sighed.

"Well, what are ye waitin' for?" asked the dragon.

"I'm just thinking," began Stan slowly. "What a pity it would be if I had to kill you with this beautiful barrel."

"What d'ye mean?" asked the dragon.

"Well, just take a look at my hands," answered Stan, holding out his hands with fingers outspread, as though there was something special about them. "D'you see those magnetic veins? Anything I throw *always comes back*, and if this barrel should collide with your head in passing, there'd be one nice cracked dragon's skull lying around."

"Oh," said the dragon nervously. "There's no great hurry for you to have your turn just yet. Let's have something to eat first. I'm feeling hungry." And he went back to his house and brought back great stacks of food and they both sat down and ate their fill, right up till evening when the moon came out.

"Well," said Stan Bolovan, standing up and stretching himself, "I suppose I ought to have my throw now, but I'd better wait till the moon goes down in the sky, because if the barrel happens to land on the moon, it's liable to get stuck there for ever. You wouldn't want to lose it, would you?"

"Oh no," said the dragon hastily. "It's me mother's favourite barrel. Better not risk throwing it yet. In fact, better not throw it at all, in case it gets stuck on some planet or other."

"But I must," protested Stan Bolovan. "Your mother distinctly said I must. It's a test of strength, remember?"

"I'll tell ye what," proposed the dragon. "Let *me* throw it back towards the house. I'll make it go farther this time and I'll tell her that you did it. Then you'll have beaten me, and Mother will never know a thing."

"No!" replied Stan emphatically. "No! No! No!"

But when the dragon offered him twenty sacks of gold not to throw the barrel, he said: "Oh, very well, if you feel so strongly about it . . ."

Then the dragon returned to the house and told his mother that Stan had beaten him once again and had thrown the barrel a good mile further than he had. "Oh dearie me," said the mother and she began to feel rather scared.

But by next morning she had another plan to get rid of Stan Bolovan.

70

"Go and fetch me water from the spring," she said giving them twenty big buffalo skins. "Let's see which of you can carry most in one day."

The dragon started first and went backwards and forwards from his house to the spring and from the spring to the house till he had filled and emptied all twenty skins. He then handed them to Stan.

"Your turn," he said.

Instead of taking them Stan took a knife out of his pocket, bent down and began scratching the earth near the spring.

"What on earth are ye up to now?" asked the dragon suspiciously.

"I want to get at this spring," replied Stan. "Then I'll carry the whole lot of water in one go..Seems a terrible waste of time going to and fro with those tiny buffalo skins."

"N—n—no," said the dragon nervously. "You mustn't do that. That spring belongs to the local dragon family. It was originally made by my great-great-great-grandfather. Keep your hands off it, please. I'll carry the skins for you in half the time I did it. Mother will be none the wiser."

"No," said Stan firmly, and went on digging.

Finally the dragon had to promise him yet another twenty sacks of gold before he could get him to stop. And so the dragon did all the to-ing and fro-ing with the skins, rushing like mad to get it finished before the day was over, while Stan lay resting on his great bed.

The mother dragon got more and more scared on learning that her son had been beaten yet again, but by the next morning she had thought of another plan.

They were told to go to collect wood in the forest, to see which of them would get more. The dragon immediately began wrenching out great oaks as if they were no bigger than matchsticks and arranged them neatly in rows. But Stan climbed to the top of a tree that had a long creeper trailing round it. With this creeper he tied the top of the tree he was sitting on to the top of the next tree.

"I'm tying all the trees together," he explained to the dragon. "Then I'll be able to clear the whole forest at one go."

"No! Please no!" wailed the dragon, his scales visibly shrinking with fear. "My great-great-great-great-grandfather planted this forest. Please, please don't."

"Sorry about that," said Stan Bolovan, "but I'm not going to trudge to and fro with a mere half dozen trees at a time."

So the dragon had to promise yet another twenty sacks of gold before Stan finally said, "Oh very well, if you insist . . ."

The dragons, mother and son, now decided they had had enough and told Stan they would give him another hundred sacks of gold if he would go away and leave them in peace.

Stan, of course, was only too delighted. But how was he going to carry all those heavy sacks of gold back to his house? That night, as he lay awake in his giant bed thinking how to solve this problem, he heard the voices of the mother dragon and her son.

"We shall be ruined," the mother was saying, "we'll have nothing left."

"Well, what is there we can do about it?" the son asked in a rather weak and helpless tone of voice.

"There's only one thing we can do," replied the mother. "You must KILL him this very night."

"*Me* kill '*im*?" exclaimed the son. "It's 'im who'll kill me, more likely."

"Not if you listen to your mother he won't," said she. "Now just wait till he's fast asleep, then go in and bash his head with great-grandfather's club."

"Aha!" thought Stan Bolovan, "so that's what they're up to!"

He crept quietly out of bed and went outside to the yard where the pigs' trough was. He filled it with earth and dragged it in on to his bed and covered it with blankets. He himself got under the bed and snored as noisily as he could.

Soon he heard the dragon tiptoe into the room, stop by the

bedside and bring down the club with a deafening thwack on to the trough. Stan stopped snoring and let out a long-drawn-out groan, as though he were dying. Shortly afterwards he crept out from under the bed and dragged the trough back to its place in the yard, leaving his bed nice and tidy.

When the dragon and his mother beheld Stan next morning, they could hardly believe their eyes.

"G—g—g—good mornin'," said the dragon. "'Ope you slept well on your last night here."

"I slept fine," replied Stan, "just fine. There was a fly or something that crawled over my nose and tickled me rather, but otherwise I slept just fine. So fine, in fact, that I think I'll stay here another night, if you don't mind. It's not all that often I get the chance to sleep in such a comfy bed."

Both mother and son looked so distinctly uncomfortable when they heard this that Stan continued: "Well, if I'm really all that unwelcome, I'll leave today. I don't wish to be a burden . . . but on one condition."

"Any condition, any condition," said both dragons hastily in unison. "You name it."

"You must carry all the sacks of gold back to my house for me. It'd look a bit undignified for the mighty Stan Bolovan to be seen lugging sacks around."

The dragon was only too eager to comply. He picked up the sacks in his great claws and flung them on to his enormous back.

"Well, I'll say cheeri-ho," said Stan to the mother dragon, "and thanks for everything."

"Not at all, not at all," she replied and hurriedly locked the door behind him.

Stan and the dragon began their long journey back home. After a trek lasting many hours, Stan could hear the sound of his children's voices in the distance.

He stopped and turned to the dragon.

"Those are my children playing and shouting. I shouldn't think you'd care to meet them. There's about a hundred of them—all just about as strong as I am, and they can be very rough sometimes. Perhaps you'd . . ." But before he could finish his sentence, the dragon had dropped the sacks and fled in terror. He didn't fancy the thought of meeting a hundred young Stan Bolovans!

Just at that moment Stan's wife came out to greet him, followed by the enormous brood of laughing, jolly children.

There was enough gold in the sacks to feed and clothe them for the rest of their lives.

Eeyore Loses a Tail and Pooh Finds One

The Old Grey Donkey, Eeyore, stood by himself in a thistly corner of the Forest, his front feet well apart, his head on one side, and thought about things. Sometimes he thought sadly to himself, "Why?" and sometimes he thought, "Wherefore?" and sometimes he thought, "Inasmuch as which?"—and sometimes he didn't quite know what he was thinking about. So when Winnie-the-Pooh came stumping along, Eeyore was very glad to be able to stop thinking for a little, in order to say "How do you do?" in a gloomy manner to him.

"And how are you?" said Winnie-the-Pooh.

Eeyore shook his head from side to side.

"Not very how," he said. "I don't seem to have felt at all how for a long time."

"Dear, dear," said Pooh, "I'm sorry about that. Let's have a look at you."

So Eeyore stood there, gazing sadly at the ground and Winnie-the-Pooh walked all round him once.

"Why, what's happened to your tail?" he said in surprise.

"What *has* happened to it?" said Eeyore.

"It isn't there!"

"Are you sure?"

"Well, either a tail *is* there or it isn't there. You can't make a mistake about it, and yours *isn't* there!"

"Then what is?"

"Nothing."

"Let's have a look," said Eeyore, and he turned slowly round to the place where his tail had been a little while ago, and then, finding that he couldn't catch it up, he turned round the other way, until he came back to where he was at first, and then he put his head down and looked between his front legs, and at last he said, with a long, sad sigh, "I believe you're right."

"Of course I'm right," said Pooh.

"That Accounts for a Good Deal," said Eeyore gloomily. "It Explains Everything. No Wonder."

"You must have left it somewhere," said Winnie-the-Pooh.

"Somebody must have taken it," said Eeyore. "How Like Them," he added, after a long silence.

Pooh felt that he ought to say something helpful about it, but didn't quite know what. So he decided to do something helpful instead.

"Eeyore," he said solemnly, "I, Winnie-the-Pooh, will find your tail for you."

"Thank you, Pooh," answered Eeyore. "You're a real friend," said he. "Not Like Some," he said.

So Winnie-the-Pooh went off to find Eeyore's tail.

It was a fine spring morning in the Forest as he started out. Little soft clouds played happily in a blue sky, skipping from time to time in front of the sun as if they had come to put it out, and then sliding away suddenly so that the next might have his turn. Through them and between them the sun shone bravely; and a copse which had worn its firs all the year round seemed old and dowdy now beside the new green lace which the beeches had put on so prettily. Through copse and spinney marched Bear; down open slopes of gorse and heather, over rocky beds of streams, up steep banks of sandstone into the heather again; and so at last, tired and hungry, to the Hundred Acre Wood. For it was in the Hundred Acre Wood that Owl lived.

"And if anyone knows anything about anything," said Bear

to himself, "it's Owl who knows something about something," he said, "or my name's not Winnie-the-Pooh," he said. "Which it is," he added. "So there you are."

Owl lived at The Chestnuts, an old-world residence of great charm, which was grander than anybody else's or seemed so to Bear, because it had both a knocker *and* a bell-pull. Underneath the knocker there was a notice which said:

PLES. RING IF AN RNSER IS REQIRD.

Underneath the bell-pull there was a notice which said:

PLEZ CNOKE IF AN RNSR IS NOT REQID.

These notices had been written by Christopher Robin, who was the only one in the forest who could spell; for Owl, wise though he was in many ways, able to read and write and spell his own name WOL, yet somehow went all to pieces over delicate words like MEASLES and BUTTEREDTOAST.

Winnie-the-Pooh read the two notices very carefully, first from left to right, and afterwards, in case he had missed some of it, from right to left. Then to make quite sure, he knocked and pulled the knocker, and he pulled and knocked the bell-rope, and he called out in a very loud voice, "Owl! I require an answer! It's Bear speaking." And the door opened and Owl looked out.

"Hallo, Pooh," he said. "How's things?"

"Terrible and Sad," said Pooh, "because Eeyore, who is a friend of mine, has lost his tail. And he's Moping about it. So could you very kindly tell me how to find it for him?"

"Well," said Owl, "the customary procedure in such cases is as follows."

"What does Crustimoney Proseedcake mean?" said Pooh. "For I am a Bear of Very Little Brain, and long words Bother me."

"It means the Thing to Do."

"As long as it means that, I don't mind," said Pooh humbly.

"The thing to do is as follows. First, Issue a Reward. Then—"

"Just a moment," said Pooh, holding up his paw. "*What* do we do to this—what you were saying? you sneezed just as you were going to tell me."

"I *didn't* sneeze."

"Yes, you did, Owl."

"Excuse me, Pooh, I didn't. You can't sneeze without knowing it."

"Well, you can't know it without something having been sneezed."

"What I *said* was, 'First *Issue* a Reward'."

"You're doing it again," said Pooh sadly.

"A Reward!" said Owl very loudly. "We write a notice to say that we will give a large something to anybody who finds Eeyore's tail."

"I see, I see," said Pooh, nodding his head. "Talking about large somethings," he went on dreamily, "I generally have a small something about now—about this time in the morning," and he looked wistfully at the cupboard in the corner of Owl's parlour; "just a mouthful of condensed milk or what-not, with perhaps a lick of honey—"

"Well then," said Owl, "we write out this notice, and we put it up all over the Forest."

"A lick of honey," murmured Bear to himself, "or—or not, as the case may be." And he gave a deep sigh, and tried very hard to listen to what Owl was saying.

But Owl went on and on, using longer and longer words, until at last he came back to where he started, and he explained that the person to write out this notice was Christopher Robin.

"It was he who wrote the ones on my front door for me. Did you see them, Pooh?"

For some time now Pooh had been saying "yes" and "no" in turn, with his eyes shut, to all that Owl was saying, and having said, "yes, yes," last time, he said, "No, not at all," now, without really knowing what Owl was talking about.

"Didn't you see them?" said Owl, a little surprised. "Come and look at them now."

So they went outside. And Pooh looked at the knocker and the notice below it, and he looked at the bell-rope and the notice below it, and the more he looked at the bell-rope, the more he felt that he had seen something like it, somewhere else, sometime before.

"Handsome bell-rope, isn't it?" said Owl.

Pooh nodded.

"It reminds me of something," he said, "but I can't think what. Where did you get it?"

"I just came across it in the Forest. It was hanging over a

bush, and I thought at first somebody lived there, so I rang it, and nothing happened, and then I rang it again very loudly, and it came off in my hand, and as nobody seemed to want it, I took it home, and—"

"Owl," said Pooh solemnly, "you made a mistake, Somebody did want it."

"Who?"

"Eeyore. My dear friend Eeyore. He was—he was fond of it."

"Fond of it?"

"Attached to it," said Winnie-the-Pooh sadly.

So with these words he unhooked it, and carried it back to Eeyore; and when Christopher Robin had nailed it on in its right place again, Eeyore frisked about the forest, waving his tail so happily that Winnie-the-Pooh came over all funny, and had to hurry home for a little snack of something to sustain him. And, wiping his mouth half an hour afterwards, he sang to himself proudly:

> *Who found the Tail?*
>   "I," said Pooh,
> "At a quarter to two
>   (Only it was quarter to eleven really),
> *I* found the Tail."

The Ju-Ju Man

In the forest the monkeys lived in the tree-tops and the
crocodiles lived in the pools and the snakes slept under thick
green leaves. In one part of the forest there was a cave made
of rock. In the cave lived a Ju-ju man. He made magic in his
cave. He could cast spells on people with his magic. He could
make people ill and he could make them well again. He could
bring good luck or he could bring bad luck. He could find things
that were lost and he could make things disappear.

The black people who lived in huts in the forest were afraid
of the Ju-ju man. They were afraid he might make them ill or
bring them bad luck. So they gave him presents to make him
like them and be kind to them.

Sometimes, outside the cave of the Ju-ju man, there would be
a bunch of ripe bananas and a bowl of plums and some fresh
fish from the river. The Ju-ju man never said thank you for all
these presents. He just ate them up and waited for the people to
bring him some more. He was very greedy and the presents did
not make him kind.

A little black girl named Lily lived in the forest. The lily
flowers that grow in the forest can be dark, almost black, as well
as white, so the name fitted her well. When she had nothing
special to do, she often hid among the bushes and watched the
door of the cave where the Ju-ju man lived. She liked to watch
him when he swept out his cave with a broom of stiff leaves. He
did this every day, after he had had his breakfast.

The Ju-Ju Man

First the Ju-ju man put all his belongings outside the cave so that he could sweep in the nooks and corners. He put out his cups and bowls, and blankets and cooking pots, and the queer things he used to make spells. While he swept the cave, Lily could look at all his things. He was very rich. He had more things in his cave than Lily and her father and mother and brothers and sisters had in their hut. He had more things than anyone else in the whole of the forest.

One evening when Lily was watching from among the bushes, a yellow lion cub padded past the cave. The Ju-ju man came to the door and said kindly:

"Good evening, yellow lion cub. Will you come in and have some supper with me? I have plenty for the two of us."

"Thank you," said the lion cub and he went into the cave.

Lily waited and waited and waited, but the lion cub never came out again.

The next time the Ju-ju man swept out his cave, Lily saw that he had something new. It was a yellow jug. She wondered where it had come from. She had never seen a jug like it in the forest.

One evening, when Lily was watching, a striped tiger strolled past the cave. The Ju-ju man came to the door and said kindly:

"Good evening, striped tiger. Will you come in and have some supper with me? I have plenty for the two of us."

"Thank you," said the tiger, and he went into the cave.

Lily waited and waited and waited, but the tiger never came out again.

The next time the Ju-ju man swept out his cave, Lily saw that he had something else new. It was a striped mat for the floor. She wondered where it had come from. She had never before seen a mat like it in the forest.

One evening, a grey monkey with a long tail frisked past the cave. The Ju-ju man came to the door and said kindly:

"Good evening, grey monkey. Will you come in and have some supper with me? I have plenty for the two of us."

"Thank you," said the grey monkey and he went into the cave.

Lily waited and waited and waited, but the monkey never came out again.

The next time the Ju-ju man swept the cave, Lily saw that he had something else new. It was a grey fur hat with a long tassel. He wore it on his head while he swept and the tassel swung to and fro. She wondered where it had come from. She had never before seen a hat like it in the forest.

One evening, a pink parrot flew by the cave. The Ju-ju man came to the door and said kindly:

"Good evening, pink parrot. Will you come in and have some supper with me? I have plenty for the two of us."

"Thank you," said the pink parrot and he went into the cave.

Lily waited and waited and waited, but the parrot never came out again.

The next time the Ju-ju man swept out his cave, Lily saw that he had something else new. It was a fan made of pink feathers. This time she did not wonder who had given it to him. She guessed what had happened. She knew he had cast a spell on the parrot and turned him into a fan.

She also guessed what had happened to the yellow lion cub and the striped tiger and the grey monkey. They had been turned into the yellow jug and the striped mat and the hat with a long tassel.

Lily made up her mind to be very careful and not to let the wicked Ju-ju man turn her into anything by his magic. But one day when she was hiding near the cave, she saw that the Ju-ju man was asleep. His eyes were shut and he was lying quite, quite still. She came out of her hiding place and tickled the sole of his foot with a blade of grass. He did not move. So she was sure he was asleep and not pretending. She crept into his cave on tiptoe to have a good look round.

Lily wanted to see the magic things he used when he put spells on people and turned them into jugs and mats and hats

83

and fans. She saw a bone in a corner. Perhaps it was a magic bone. She was just going to touch it when the Ju-ju man sat up and grabbed her with his skinny black hands.

"Little black girl," he said kindly, "will you have supper with me? I have plenty for the two of us."

"No thank you," said Lily. "I have had my supper."

"Never mind about that!" said the Ju-ju man. "You can stay here with me and have some more of my supper. You must. Or I shall have to make you."

"Very well," said Lily, who knew she could not get away from the Ju-ju man, he was too strong and cunning.

The Ju-ju man began to stir the broth which was cooking on the fire. While he stirred, Lily looked round the cave.

"You have some nice things in your cave," said Lily. "I think you must have everything you need."

"I have almost all I need," said the Ju-ju man. "There's just one thing I want. That is a stool to sit on while I stir my broth."

"What kind of a stool?" asked Lily.

"A little black stool," said the Ju-ju man.

Then Lily knew that she must be very careful indeed because the Ju-ju man was going to turn her into a black stool. So she watched everything he did very closely.

When the broth was cooked, he put some into two bowls. And when he thought Lily was not looking, he put a pinch of powder into one bowl and whispered some magic words. He gave this bowl to Lily, and kept the other for himself. But when he was fetching two spoons, and his back was turned, Lily changed the bowls round. She gave him the one with the powder in it.

"Eat up your broth! Eat it up like a good girl!" said the Ju-ju man, rubbing his skinny hands together.

"It is too hot," said Lily.

"Then blow on it," said the Ju-ju man.

So Lily blew on her broth to cool it.

"Now eat it up! Spoon it up!" said the Ju-ju man, dancing

84

up and down.

"I don't know how to use a spoon," said Lily. "Please show me. We haven't any spoons in our hut."

"Watch me," said the Ju-ju man. "Hold the handle like this. Dip the other end in like this. Lift it up. And drink." He drank a spoonful to show her.

"Show me again," begged Lily, and the Ju-ju man drank another spoonful, and she tried to copy him. But her hand was shaking so much that she spilt the broth on the floor.

"Hurry up! Hurry up!" said the Ju-ju man. "Let's have a race to see who can finish first." Lily ate as fast as she could, but her hand was still shaking and the Ju-ju man was winning easily.

But when the Ju-ju man had eaten half his broth, he began to shrink and shrink. He grew smaller and smaller. His head got flatter and flatter. His legs got shorter and shorter. Soon he had turned into a little black stool.

Then Lily looked round the cave and found a pot of the magic powder that the Ju-ju man had sprinkled on the soup. She put a pinch on the jug and the mat and the hat and the fan, and they turned back into the lion cub and the tiger and the monkey and the parrot.

Then they all danced for joy and ran home to their mothers. And though the Ju-ju man was now only a black stool, and quite safe, they never went near his cave again.

THE JU-JU MAN

A pinch of his powder,
A sip of his tea,
And you'll be in his power,
And never get free.

He'll turn you to something
He needs for his hut,
It might be an ear-ring,
A flower or a nut.

So if he should beckon
And ask you inside,
Run away in the forest!
Find somewhere to hide!

The Sparrows' Tug-of-War

<hr>

One summer morning Mother Sparrow was sitting on her nest full of eggs, enjoying the bright summer sunshine. She could hear the other birds chirping merrily away among the trees and the monkeys chattering for all their worth. In fact everything would have been perfect but for one thing —Father Sparrow was cross, very cross.

"It's that ugly old crocodile," he grumbled. "I went down to bathe in that nice shallow part of the river, you know, and there he was, spread out all over the place. No room for me at all! And when I very politely told him off, he opened his big mouth and laughed. And do you know what he said? 'Go away,' he said, 'I shall stay here as long as I please. Go and have your dip somewhere else'."

Just as Father Sparrow was speaking, there was a sudden tremendous bump against the tree which tipped him off his twig and very nearly flung Mother Sparrow out of her nest. Father Sparrow flew up to see who it was. It was none other than Brother Elephant taking his morning constitutional. "Hey there, Brother Elephant," called out Father Sparrow with a furious chirrup. "D'you realise that you've nearly shaken my missus out of her nest?"

"Well what of that, there's no harm done," answered Brother Elephant, without even apologising.

"No harm done indeed! You've given her the shock of her life. I warn you, Brother Elephant, if you ever do that again,

I'll tie you up!"

Brother Elephant gave a mighty guffaw. "Ho! Ho! Ho! Tie me up indeed! Go ahead, Father Sparrow. You and all the other sparrows. You are perfectly welcome to tie me up. *But you won't keep me tied.* Neither you nor all the sparrows in the whole wide world." And off he stamped, still guffawing.

"We'll see about that," twittered Father Sparrow, his feathers all a-fluff. Still furiously angry, he flew down to the river where he found the crocodile still all a-sprawl, sunning himself in the nice shallow part of the river.

"I give you warning, Crocodile," chirped Father Sparrow sternly (whereupon the crocodile lazily opened one eye), "that if you are not out of this place by tomorrow morning, *I shall tie you up.*"

"Tie me up as much as you like," answered the crocodile, closing his eye, "and welcome to it. *But you can't keep me tied—* neither you nor all the sparrows in the whole wide world."

"We'll see about that," said Father Sparrow and whisking his tail he flew back to Mother Sparrow.

All the rest of the day he was very busy discussing matters with all the other sparrows in the forest. And in the afternoon, several hundreds of them got together and, working very hard, they finally made a long length of creeper, very thick and very stout—as strong as any rope.

Soon Brother Elephant came crashing through the forest and, Doing! came bump against Father Sparrow's tree.

"And now what are you going to do, Father Sparrow?" asked Brother Elephant. "Ready to tie me up, eh?"

"Yes we are," replied Father Sparrow. And he and all his friends flew up and round and round and down and up again with the long creeper-rope between their beaks, till it was all tightly bound round Brother Elephant's enormous body.

"Now listen to me, Brother Elephant," said Father Sparrow, "when I give the word 'PULL', pull as hard as you can."

"Rightee-ho," answered Brother Elephant, guffawing and

shaking with laughter.

But all the sparrows had flown away with the other end of the creeper-rope, pulling it through bush and tree, till they came to the river where Crocodile was.

"So you've come to tie me up, Father Sparrow?" he asked, opening a lazy eye.

"Yes, that's exactly what we *are* going to do," came the reply.

"Tie away," said Crocodile and the sparrows set to work pecking and tugging, flying up and down and up and down again and again and round and round, till the rope was tight and firm round Crocodile's long, slimy body.

"Now," said Father Sparrow, "when I say 'PULL', don't forget, *pull*."

"Right," said Crocodile, half asleep, and the sparrows whisked their tails and flew off.

Then Father Sparrow perched himself in the middle of the creeper-rope where neither Brother Elephant nor Crocodile could see him (and neither of *them* could see the other), and then, IN A VERY LOUD CHIRP, he called "PULL".

You can well imagine Crocodile's surprise when he found himself jerked out of his sleep and half-way up the river bank. You can also imagine Brother Elephant's astonishment when, a couple of seconds later, *he* found himself pulled off his feet— by Crocodile tugging back. Of course, they both thought it was Father Sparrow who was pulling them.

"What a mighty sparrow!" thought Brother Elephant.

"That little bird certainly knows how to pull!" thought Crocodile.

And so now the tug-of-war began in earnest. They each pulled with all their might and main. Sometimes Brother Elephant would gain the upper hand for a few minutes and Crocodile would be dragged up the river bank. Sometimes Crocodile would pull more strongly and Brother Elephant would have to dig his big feet into the earth to stop himself being pulled over. The contest was pretty even, and it went on and on with both of them puffing and panting and groaning, and all the sparrows watching from up above twittered and laughed and enjoyed themselves hugely.

Towards evening, when the sun was beginning to set, Crocodile said to himself, "I'd better not let the other animals see me in this state when they come down to drink at the river." So he called out: "Oh, please, Father Sparrow, please stop tugging and untie me. I promise never to take your bathing place again."

And Brother Elephant cried out in a tiny trumpet: "Father Sparrow, if you stop pulling and untie me, I promise I will never bump into your tree again."

"Oh very well," said Father Sparrow, "very well."

And so all the sparrows set to work again, hopping and pulling and pecking and chattering, until they had untied Crocodile, who then slid, shamefaced, into the river among the tall reeds and hid himself until it was pitch dark. Then they went and did the same thing to Brother Elephant who then trod quietly away (almost on tip-toe!), thoroughly ashamed of being beaten by such a tiny bird. And all the sparrows, satisfied with their day's work, whisked their tails and flew away.

And Father Sparrow was now able to live in peace and take his dip in his favourite shallow part of the river. And Mother Sparrow was able to sit quietly on her nest of eggs.

The Brave Little Tailor

◇

There was a lovely plate of white bread and jam on the little table next to the tailor as he sat sewing on that very hot summer day. But the trouble was it was *so* hot that lots of horrible flies kept buzzing round and landing on the bread and jam.

"Confound them!" cried the little tailor, and he got so impatient that he lifted his damp ironing-cloth and brought it down with a great swish on top of them. When he took the cloth away, there were seven dead flies scattered on the table and plate.

"Aha!" cried the little tailor triumphantly. "Seven at one blow! What a hero I am!" And he straightway set to work to make himself a belt, and on it he wrote the words: SEVEN AT ONE BLOW.

As he gazed at these brave words, written in very large letters, the tailor felt very proud of himself.

"Seven at one blow," he thought to himself. "I must go out into the world and show what a great hero I am. I cannot spend the rest of my days in this tiny town." So he set out the next morning with a chunk of cheese in his pocket and his pet bird on his wrist, whistling a merry tune as he walked gaily along.

Very soon he met a huge giant who was taller than any of the houses along the street.

"Would you care to accompany me on my travels?" the tailor called out to him. "Just look at this," he continued, pointing to his belt. "Seven at one blow—that's what I've done. That's how strong I am."

The huge giant looked down at the little tailor with tremendous scorn.

"Strong!" he bawled. "Strong! D'you call that strong! We'll soon see how strong you are." And he picked up a large stone and squeezed it till water dripped from it. "Can you do that?" he asked. "Can you do that, little man?"

"That's nothing," said the little tailor airily and he took the hunk of cheese out of his pocket and squeezed it till the whey oozed freely from it.

The giant grunted. He looked round for another large stone, picked it up and threw it up high into the clouds.

"Let's just see whether you can do that," he said.

"I notice that your stone came back down again, even though it went up into the clouds," remarked the little tailor. "When I throw mine up, you'll never see it again." And he threw his little pet bird up into the sky. Of course, the little creature was so glad to find itself soaring high in the sky that it flew far away, never to return.

The giant grunted even more at this. He pointed to a huge tree that had fallen across the way and said, "Let's see how hard you can work without getting tired. Just carry this tree with me."

"Right," said the little tailor briskly. "I'd better take the heavier end where all the thick branches are," and he very nimbly slipped among the leaves where he was completely hidden from view, so that the giant carried both tree and tailor without knowing it. The giant strode along for a while with his enormous burden but he soon got tired and dropped the tree to the ground with a tremendous groan.

The little tailor jumped noiselessly out.

"Tired already?" he asked. "I'm as fresh as a daisy!" And whistling gaily the little tailor walked briskly beside the giant, who was still groaning.

They kept going for some time, the little tailor humming and whistling cheerfully all the time and the giant looking more and more worried. Suddenly his huge face lit up.

"D'you see that apple tree over there?" he asked. "Come and help yourself to a few rosy ones." And so saying he stretched out his long arm, pulled down a branch and called, "Catch!" The little tailor was taken by surprise. He couldn't hold the branch down, of course, and when the giant let go he was flung high up into the air and came down again with a mighty bump.

"So you couldn't manage to hold that tiny twig?" said the giant. "You are a weakling, aren't you?"

The little tailor had recovered his wits.

"I was merely jumping over the top of the tree—to avoid that man with the gun, over there. He was about to fire and I got out of his way just in time." He said all this very coolly.

This made the giant angrier than ever. "I'll get even with this little dwarf yet," he muttered to himself.

"Would you like to spend the night in my cave?" he called down. The tailor accepted very politely and they were soon inside a deep, dark cave where there were ten giants eating whole sheep with their fingers. The giant pointed to a bed big enough for fifty tailors and wished him goodnight. When he was alone, the tailor took the pillow off the bed and lay down on it. Even the pillow was very much bigger than an ordinary bed and gave the tailor ample room.

In the dead of night the giant came in and gave the bed a mighty whack with a stout stick. "Well, that's the end of that little boaster," he muttered. "Seven at one blow, indeed!" Then he went back to bed. But as soon as he had gone, the little tailor crept out of his pillow-bed and set off on his travels again, as cheerful as ever. He had not gone far when he met seven smart Soldiers of the King. One of them saw the words SEVEN AT ONE BLOW on the tailor's belt and he called them all to a halt.

"Hey you," he called out, "you'll be mighty useful to our

King if you can fight as well as you claim. Come along with us."
And so the little tailor marched along with the seven smart
Soldiers of the King.

The King was indeed delighted with this doughty new
recruit and he said to the tailor: "There are two monster giants
killing and robbing my people. If you can get rid of them, you
shall marry the Princess, my daughter, and have half my
kingdom."

"That will be well within my powers, Your Majesty," replied
the little tailor and he immediately set off in search of the two
giants. He found them asleep under a tree in the forest. They
were snoring so powerfully that the trees shook, as though in a
storm, every time they breathed. The tailor filled a bag of
stones and climbed up into a tree. He threw a stone at one of
the giants and caught him beautifully right on the tip of his
nose. He awoke in a fury and roared at the other one: "How
dare you bang me on the nose!"

"I don't know what on earth you are talking about," replied
the other. "I did nothing of the kind." They quarrelled and
argued violently for quite some time but finally went off to sleep
again. This time the little tailor threw a stone and hit the
second giant on the nose. He jumped up in a great rage and
roared, "So you are having your revenge after all, are you?"
They both got on their feet and began fighting each other
hammer and tongs. They wrenched huge trees out of the ground
to use as weapons and the end of it was that they killed each
other.

The little tailor then got down from the tree and went back
to the King to claim his reward.

"Not just yet, brave little tailor," replied His Majesty. "There
is one more task I must ask you to perform. There is a unicorn
running wild in the forest and I want you to bring it back alive
to me."

"Only one, Your Majesty?" said the little tailor coolly. "I'll
catch seven if you like."

So off he went back to the forest, but this time he took with him a long coil of rope and an axe. He espied the unicorn from afar; it was making straight for him with its horn sticking out of its forehead like a spear.

The tailor stood firm in its path until the very last second and then skipped aside so that the unicorn careered on and got its horn stuck deep in the trunk of a tree. The tailor wound the rope round its neck and chopped away the part of the trunk where the beast had its horn stuck fast. Then he marched it in triumph back to the palace.

The King was pleased but he still would not give the tailor his just reward.

"There's one last thing you must do," said the King. "You must catch the wild boar that is killing my woodcutters."

"Only one?" asked the little tailor airily, and off he went once more, humming and whistling, and refusing the offer of help from the King's huntsmen. But when he saw the terrible boar with its savage tusks, he had a bit of a fright and ran away as fast as he could until he came to a little chapel where the door was open. In he rushed, with the boar thundering after him. But the little tailor, recovering his wits, sprang through a tiny window and then came back round and firmly locked the chapel door. The boar was now a prisoner and the tailor went back to tell the King of his capture.

This time the King could not refuse his reward, so the little tailor who had killed SEVEN AT ONE BLOW married the Princess and in due time became King himself.

The Tiger, the Brahmin and the Jackal

◆

The people of a tiny village in India were very angry with a certain tiger who used to come marauding among their poor homes every evening. One night several of their brave men went out with a large net, caught him and locked him fast in a cage, where they left him snarling his lungs out.

One day a Brahmin happened to be walking along close by and he heard the terrible noise. When he got near the cage, the Tiger cried out, "Oh brother Brahmin, brother Brahmin! have pity on me. Please unlock this cage so that I may go and quench my thirst in the stream."

The Brahmin was terrified. "Brother Tiger," he said, "if I let you out will you not eat me?"

"Oh, indeed to goodness no, I will not," replied the Tiger. "How could I possibly be so ungrateful to one who has saved my life? All I want is a little drink of water."

So the Brahmin opened the door of the cage. But no sooner was the Tiger outside than he said, "Now I am going to eat you. And then I shall have a refreshing drink."

"Oh, Brother Tiger," pleaded the Brahmin, quivering with terror, "what about your promise? And, besides, is it right that you should eat me when I have just set you free?"

"It is both right and fair," replied the Tiger. "I am now going to eat you."

"*Please* do not act in haste," implored the Brahmin. "Let us first seek the opinions of five of our brothers and if they all agree

that it is right and fair that you should eat me, then I am willing to die."

"Very well," said the Tiger, "so be it."

So the Brahmin and the Tiger walked along together till they came to a Banyan Tree.

"Brother Banyan," said the Brahmin, "is it right and fair that Brother Tiger should eat me after I have set him free from his cage?"

The Banyan Tree replied in a slow, gloomy tone: "When the sun is hot in high summer, men come and rest in the cool of my shady branches. But in the evening, when they are no longer hot and weary, they get up and break my twigs and scatter my leaves. They show no gratitude. I say, let the Tiger eat the Brahmin."

The Tiger was pleased with this but the Brahmin said: "That is only one opinion. We have yet to ask another four."

So they walked on for a while until they met a camel.

"Brother Camel," said the Brahmin, "do you find it right and fair that Brother Tiger should eat me when I set him free from his cage?"

The Camel replied in lazy tones: "In my young days when I worked with all the vigour of my youthful body, my master took good care of me and fed me well. But now when I am old he makes me work harder than ever before, places heavy burdens on my back and beats me when I am weary. There is no justice among men. I say, let the Tiger eat the Brahmin."

The Tiger was about to pounce upon the Brahmin, but the latter reminded him that there were still three opinions to be heard, and so they continued to walk until, after a while, they saw an eagle flying above their heads.

The Brahmin called out to him, "Brother Eagle, Brother Eagle! Does it seem right and fair to you that Brother Tiger should eat me when I have just let him free from his cage?"

The Eagle paused in his flight and soared low above them.

"I am a bird of the skies," he replied, "and do no harm to

any man. Yet men come and rob my nest and shoot at me with their murderous weapons. Men are cruel creatures. Therefore I say, let the Tiger eat the Brahmin."

The Tiger was more ready than ever to spring upon the Brahmin but the Brahmin again reminded him that there were still two opinions to be heard.

So on they walked until by and by they came to a river bank where an alligator was basking in the sun.

"Oh, Brother Alligator," implored the Brahmin. "Tell us whether you judge that it is right and fair that Brother Tiger should eat me in return for my kindness in setting him free from captivity."

The Alligator replied without even turning his head: "When men approach the river bank I have to hide in the water, for they are for ever trying to catch me and kill me. They give me no peace. My judgement is, let the Tiger eat the Brahmin."

The Tiger purred with glee but the Brahmin still had hope and told the Tiger to have patience until they had heard the fifth and final opinion.

After walking some distance further they came upon a jackal.

"Brother Jackal, oh, Brother Jackal," cried the Brahmin in his most imploring voice. "Is it right and fair that Brother Tiger should eat me when I have given him his freedom?"

The Jackal looked puzzled. "Pray tell me what this is all about," he said.

"I found Brother Tiger locked up in a cage," the Brahmin explained, "and he asked me to let him out so that he could quench his thirst in a nearby stream. But no sooner was he out of the cage than he wanted to eat me."

"What kind of cage was it?" asked the Jackal.

"A large, iron cage," replied the Brahmin.

"And you let him out of this large, iron cage?"

"Yes, Brother Jackal," answered the Brahmin.

"I really do not understand. I do not understand this at all," said the Jackal. "You will have to take me to the spot where this cage is, so that I may see it for myself."

So the Tiger, the Brahmin and the Jackal all walked back to the place where the large, iron cage stood.

"Now, let me see," said the Jackal, walking slowly round the cage and examining it very carefully. "Where were you exactly at the beginning of this whole affair?"

"I was simply here on the roadside wending my way along," replied the Brahmin.

"And you, Tiger, where were you?" asked the Jackal.

"I was inside the cage," replied the Tiger.

"Please bear with me a little longer," continued the Jackal. "I still have not got a clear picture of the situation. Would you be so very kind as to show me where exactly you were in the cage. In the front of the cage, perhaps, or at the back, or just prowling around in the middle."

"If you *must* know," said the Tiger with some show of impatience, "I was standing just here, on this precise spot," and he walked into the cage to show the Jackal exactly where he had been when the Brahmin was passing.

"Oh, thank you, Tiger, that makes the matter much clearer," said the Jackal. "But forgive me if I press for a few more details. I still fail to understand why you did not come out of the cage by yourself."

"The door was shut," replied the Tiger briefly.

"Oh yes, of course, of course," mused the Jackal. "By the way, how does this cage-door shut?"

"It shuts like this," said the Brahmin, pushing the door to.

"And does this particular door lock?" enquired the Jackal. "And if it does, does it lock from the outside or from the inside?"

"It locks like this," said the Brahmin. And he bolted the door of the cage.

Then the Jackal said, "Now that the door is shut and bolted, Brother Brahmin, I think it advisable to leave it so." And he cried out to the Tiger, "You, Tiger, are a wicked and ungrateful creature. When the kind Brahmin let you out to quench your thirst, you were ready to eat him in return for his good deed. I hope no one will ever set you free again."

And to the Brahmin the Jackal said: "Farewell, Brother Brahmin. Go on your way in peace." And he ran off leaving the Brahmin a happy and grateful man.

Mr. Miacca

◆

Tommy Grimes was sometimes a good boy, and sometimes a bad boy; and when he was a bad boy, he was a very bad boy. Now his mother used to say to him: "Tommy, Tommy, be a good boy, and don't go out of the street, or else Mr. Miacca will take you." But still when he was a bad boy he would go out of the street; and one day, sure enough, he had scarcely got round the corner, when Mr. Miacca did catch him and popped him into a bag upside down, and took him off to his house.

When Mr. Miacca got Tommy inside, he pulled him out of the bag and sat him down, and felt his arms and legs. "You're rather tough," says he; "but you're all I've got for supper, and you'll not taste bad boiled. But body o' me, I've forgot the herbs, and it's bitter you'll taste without herbs. Sally! Here, I say, Sally!" and he called Mrs. Miacca.

So Mrs. Miacca came out of another room and said: "What d'ye want, my dear?"

"Oh, here's a little boy for supper," said Mr. Miacca, "and I've forgot the herbs. Mind him, will ye, while I go for them."

"All right, my love," says Mrs. Miacca, and off he goes.

Then Tommy Grimes said to Mrs. Miacca: "Does Mr. Miacca always have little boys for supper?"

"Mostly, my dear," said Mrs. Miacca, "if little boys are bad enough, and get in his way."

"And don't you have anything else but boy-meat? No pud-

ding?" asked Tommy.

"Ah, I loves pudding," says Mrs. Miacca. "But it's not often the likes of me gets pudding."

"Why, my mother is making a pudding this very day," said Tommy Grimes, "and I'm sure she'd give you some, if I ask her. Shall I run and get some?"

"Now that's a thoughtful boy," said Mrs. Miacca, "only don't be long and be sure to be back for supper."

So off Tommy pelted, and right glad he was to get off so cheap; and for many a long day he was as good as good could be, and never went round the corner of the street. But he couldn't always be good; and one day he went round the corner, and as luck would have it, he hadn't scarcely got round it when

Mr. Miacca grabbed him up, popped him in his bag, and took him home.

When he got him there, Mr. Miacca dropped him out; and when he saw him, he said: "Ah, you're the youngster that served me and my missus such a shabby trick, leaving us without any supper. Well, you shan't do it again. I'll watch over you myself. Here, get under the sofa, and I'll sit on it and watch the pot boil for you."

So poor Tommy Grimes had to creep under the sofa, and Mr. Miacca sat on it and waited for the pot to boil. And they waited and they waited, but still the pot didn't boil, till at last Mr. Miacca got tired of waiting, and he said: "Here, you under there, I'm not going to wait any longer; put out your leg, and I'll stop your giving us the slip."

So Tommy put out a leg and Mr. Miacca got a chopper, and chopped it off, and pops it in the pot.

Suddenly he calls out: "Sally, my dear, Sally!" and nobody answered. So he went into the next room to look for Mrs. Miacca, and while he was there Tommy crept out from under the sofa and ran out of the door. For it was a leg of the sofa that he had put out.

So Tommy Grimes ran home, and he never went round the corner again till he was old enough to go alone.

The Chatterbox

◆

Once upon a time there lived a young man and his young wife, Tatiana. The wife was a terrible gossip, and she couldn't keep a thing to herself. As soon as she heard a piece of news the whole village knew about it at once.

One day the man went to the forest and began to dig out a wolves' lair, and there he found a treasure. He thought to himself: "Now what shall I do? As soon as my wife knows about this, the whole district will ring with the news: they'll hear about it in every house for miles. It will get to our master's ears and then I can say goodbye to the treasure—it'll have to go to him."

He thought for a long time and finally he hit upon a plan. He buried the treasure in the earth, took careful note of the spot, and started off for home. When he came to the river, he examined the fishnet he had set there the day before and found a fine perch caught in it. He pulled it out and went on his way. Then he came to the trap he had set in the forest and there was a hare caught in it. He loosed the hare and put the perch in the trap; and he took the hare back to the river and pushed it into the net.

When he got home, he said to his wife:

"Well, Tatiana, heat the oven and bake as many pancakes as you can."

"Have you gone mad?" said his wife. "Whoever heard of heating the oven at night? And who'll want to eat pancakes so late?"

"Don't argue, just do as you're told," said the man. "I've found a treasure in the forest and we must bring it home after dark."

At this good news, Tatiana began to warm the oven and bake the pancakes.

"Eat dearest husband, eat them while they're hot."

The man ate one pancake and slipped two or three into his sack. Then he ate another one and did the same thing again; his wife didn't notice what he was doing.

"You seem to be very hungry today! I can't make the pancakes fast enough," she said to him.

"Well, it's a long way to go and the treasure is heavy, so I must eat my fill."

When he had filled up his sack with pancakes he said, "I've had enough. Now have some yourself, but hurry, for we must be on our way." So she ate as many pancakes as she wanted, and then they set out together.

The night was dark. The man walked on a little ahead of his wife, and as he went he hung the pancakes he had slipped into his sack on to the branches of the trees.

His wife saw the pancakes on the trees.

"Look, look," she cried, "there are pancakes growing on the trees!"

"Why not? There's nothing odd in that! Didn't you see the pancake cloud that passed a minute ago?"

"No, I saw nothing, I was too busy watching my feet and finding my way among the roots."

"Come along," called the man, "there's a trap here for a hare; let's have a look at it."

They got to the trap and the man pulled out the perch.

"Oh, husband dear, how could a fish get into a snare?"

"Did you not know that there are perches that can walk?" he said.

"Indeed I didn't!" said Tatiana. "Had I not seen it with my own eyes, I wouldn't have believed it!"

They came to the river and Tatiana said:

"Your net is here somewhere. I wonder if there are any fish in it?"

"We may as well look," said he.

So they dragged out the net and there they found the hare. Tatiana raised her hands to heaven.

"Oh, Lord!" she cried. "What's the world coming to? A hare in a net!"

"You silly young thing, what's so surprising in that? Haven't you ever seen a water-hare?"

"That's just the point," she said, "I haven't."

By this time they had come to the spot where he had buried the treasure. The man dug it up and filled his and his wife's sacks with gold, and they turned back towards home. Their path ran near the master's house. As they came near the house they heard the bleating of sheep.

"Oh, how dreadful!" said Tatiana, who by now was frightened of her own shadow. "What is it?"

Her husband replied:

"Run! Run for your life! It's the fiends of hell tormenting our

master! Don't let them see us!"

They ran home, panting. The man hid the gold, and they went to sleep.

"Now be careful, Tatiana, not a word to anyone about the treasure or harm will come to us."

"Of course, dear husband," she replied. "Be sure I will say nothing."

Next day they got up late. The wife lit a good fire and when the blue smoke began to curl up the chimney she took her pails and went to fetch some water. At the well the other women were also getting water and said to her:

"Your stove is lit very late today, Tatiana."

"Oh, my dears," she said, "I've been up all night; that's why I slept late."

"What were you doing at night then?"

"My husband found a treasure and we went to fetch the gold after dark."

That day the whole village rang with the tale of how Tatiana and her husband had found a treasure and carried home two sacks of gold.

Towards dusk the news reached the ears of their master. He ordered Tatiana's husband to his house.

"How dare you hide from me this treasure you found on my land?" he said.

"I know nothing of any treasure," replied the man.

"Don't lie to me!" cried the master. "I know everything. It's your own wife who has spread the news."

"But, Honourable Master, she's not right in the head!" Tatiana's husband said. "She imagines things!"

"We'll soon see about that!"

And the master summoned Tatiana.

"Did your husband find a treasure?"

"Yes, he did, sir, indeed he did."

"And did you both go at night to fetch the gold?"

"We did, sir, yes we did."

"Tell me all that happened."

"First we went through the forest, and there were pancakes hanging on the trees. . . ."

"Pancakes on the trees?"

"Why, yes, out of the pancake cloud! Then we saw the hare's trap and found a perch in it. We took the perch and went on towards the river and there we pulled out the net—and lo and behold it had caught a hare! We let him go. Not far from the river was the treasure. We filled our sacks with gold and went home. And just at that time, as we were passing near your house, we heard the fiends of hell tormenting your lordship."

At this point the master could bear it no longer, and he stamped his foot.

"Get out of my sight, you stupid woman!"

"You see," said the man, "you really can't believe a word she says."

"Yes, I see that very well. You can go."

They went home and the two of them had enough to live on ever after, so clever had the young man been with his gossiping wife.

Axe Soup

---◆---

Once upon a long time ago there was a handsome young soldier. He had fought in the wars for many a long year and was now on his way home. He was feeling tired and hungry and was just about to lie down in the woods to rest his weary legs when he espied a wooden house in the distance. He dragged himself up to the door and knocked. There was no reply, so he knocked again. There was still no reply, so he turned the knob and pushed the door open. It all looked so cosy and comfortable inside and there was such a delicious smell of food that he felt very tempted to walk in and help himself. Just then a little old woman appeared.

"Good-day to you," said the soldier. "Excuse me for arriving so unexpectedly. I did knock but there was no answer. I am so hungry, I could eat an ox. I haven't touched a morsel of food for two days."

The old woman looked at the soldier but said not a word.

"Could you perhaps offer me just a little soup?" asked the soldier, "and then I'll be on my way again."

After a very long pause the woman said slowly, "I am very poor, I have no food in the house to offer you."

The young soldier was not only handsome. He was clever too. He could smell the food, so he knew the old woman was not telling the truth.

"I'll tell you what," he said, "I could make you a really delicious soup out of my old axe here." And he pointed to the rather rusty thing slung over his shoulder. "You just find me a saucepan and fill it with water and I'll do the rest."

The old woman went and brought him what he asked for. The soldier placed the saucepan on the fire and then just sat and waited. The old woman also sat down and watched him with great curiosity.

After a while the soldier carefully put his axe into the saucepan, sat down and waited again. A few minutes later he put a spoon in the saucepan and tasted the soup.

"Not bad," he said licking his lips, "but I think we need a little salt. I don't suppose you have a spot about the house somewhere?"

The old woman got up with surprising agility and soon came back with a bowl of salt.

"Here, soldier," she said, "take as much as you need." The soldier sprinkled some into the saucepan, sat down again and waited. Then, after a few more minutes, he got up and again dipped the spoon into the water and tasted it.

"It's a lot better now," he said thoughtfully, "but I think I could improve it if I only had a spot of cabbage to add to it."

The old woman jumped up and almost ran out, soon to return with a nice healthy-looking cabbage. The soldier placed the cabbage in the saucepan, sat down and waited. A few minutes later he dipped his spoon into the soup and tasted it.

"Fine," he said, "but a few potatoes would make it even tastier."

The old woman lost no time getting an armful of potatoes which the soldier peeled and threw into the saucepan.

This went on until the soldier, by the same means, had also put butter and pepper into the soup. Then he tried it again.

"What's it like now?" asked the old woman.

"Well, it's really wonderfully tasty," replied the soldier. "A pity we haven't a bit of meat. That would really give it that extra bit of flavour." The old woman ran to her larder and returned with a hunk of good red meat which the soldier placed

in the saucepan.

"We shall soon have a soup fit for a king," he said rubbing his hands and sniffing the appetising fumes that rose from the boiling water. "Let's just wait a wee while longer for my axe-juice to really work."

Finally the soldier decided the soup was ready. The old

114

woman fetched two large soup-bowls and poured out a handsome portion into each one.

The old woman was so delighted with the taste that she brought out a loaf of bread and also a bottle of red wine. They both really enjoyed themselves.

"When do you think the axe will be ready for us to eat?" the old woman suddenly inquired.

"Well, I don't really think it's tender enough yet," replied the soldier thoughtfully. "And as I'm in a hurry to get back home to my old mother, I think I'd better take it along with me, as we'll be needing it at home."

The old woman gave him a very shrewd look but said nothing. Perhaps she understood what he had been up to. Who knows?

Anyway, the soldier got up, thanked her heartily and went on his way.

The Wonderful Tar-Baby

O ne day Brer Fox went to work and got him some tar, and mixed it with some turpentine, and fix up a contraption what he called a Tar-Baby, and he took this here Tar-Baby and set her in the big road; and then he lay off in the bushes for to see what the news was going to be. And he didn't have to wait long, neither, 'cause by and by here comes Brer Rabbit, pacing down the road—lippity-clippity, clippity-lippity—just as saucy as a jay-bird. Brer Fox, he lay low. Brer Rabbit came prancing along till he spy the Tar-Baby, and then he fetched up on his behind legs like he was 'stonished. The Tar-Baby, she sat there, she did, and Brer Fox, he lay low.

"Morning!" says Brer Rabbit, says he—"Nice weather, this morning," says he.

Tar-Baby ain't saying nothing, and Brer Fox, he lay low.

"How are your symptoms this morning?" says Brer Rabbit, says he.

Brer Fox, he wink his eye slow, and lay low, and the Tar-Baby, she ain't saying nothing.

"How you come on then? Is you deaf?" says Brer Rabbit, says he. "'Cause if you is, I can holler louder," says he.

Tar-Baby stay still, and Brer Fox, he lay low.

"You're stuck up, that's what you is," says Brer Rabbit, says he, "and I'm going to cure you, that's what I'm a-going to do," says he.

Brer Fox, he sort of chuckle in his stomach, but Tar-Baby

ain't saying nothing.

"I'm going to learn you how to talk to 'spectable folks, if it's the last act I do," says Brer Rabbit, says he. "If you don't take off that hat and tell me howdy, I'm going to bust you wide open," says he.

Tar-Baby stay still, and Brer Fox, he lay low.

Brer Rabbit keep on asking him, and the Tar-Baby, she keep on saying nothing, till presently Brer Rabbit draw back with his fist, he did, and blip! he took her on the side of the head. His fist stuck and he can't pull loose. The tar held him. But Tar-Baby, she stay still, and Brer Fox, he lay low.

"If you don't let me loose, I'll knock you again," says Brer Rabbit, says he, and with that he fetch her a wipe with the other hand, and that stuck. Tar-Baby, she ain't saying nothing, and Brer Fox, he lay low.

"Turn me loose, before I kick the natural stuffing out of you," says Brer Rabbit, says he, but the Tar-Baby, she ain't saying nothing. She just held on, and then Brer Rabbit lose the use of his feet the same way. Brer Fox, he lay low. Then Brer Rabbit squall out that if the Tar-Baby don't turn him loose, he butt her lop-sided. And then he butted, and his head got stuck. Then Brer Fox, he sauntered forth, looking just as innocent as a mocking-bird.

"Howdy, Brer Rabbit," says Brer Fox, says he. "You look sort of stuck-up this morning," says he, and then he rolled on the ground, and laughed and laughed until he couldn't laugh no more.

And that's how Brer Fox got the better of Brer Rabbit. Now you will hear how Brer Rabbit got his revenge.

Brer Rabbit He's a Good Fisherman

<hr/>

One day, when Brer Rabbit, and Brer Fox, and Brer Coon, and Brer Bear and a whole lot of them was clearing a new ground for to plant a roasting-pear patch, the sun began to get sort of hot, and Brer Rabbit, he got tired; but he didn't let on, 'cause he feared the others would call him lazy, and he keep on carrying away rubbish and piling it up, till by and by he holler out that he got a thorn in his hand, and then he take and slip off and hunt for a cool place to rest. After a while he come across a well with a bucket hanging in it.

"That looks cool," says Brer Rabbit, says he. "And cool I 'specs she is. I'll just about get in there and take a nap," and with that, in he jump, he did, and he ain't no sooner fix himself than the bucket begin to go down. Brer Rabbit, he was mighty scared. He know where he come from, but he don't know where he's going. Suddenly he feel the bucket hit the water, and there she sat, but Brer Rabbit, he keep mighty still, 'cause he don't know what minute's going to be the next. He just lay there and shook and shiver.

Brer Fox always got one eye on Brer Rabbit, and when he slip off from the new ground, Brer Fox, he sneak after him. He knew Brer Rabbit was after some project or another, and he took and crope off, he did, and watch him. Brer Fox see Brer Rabbit come to the top of the well and stop, and then he see him jump in the bucket, and then, lo and behold! he see him go down out of sight. Brer Fox was the most 'stonished fox that

you ever laid eyes on. He sat down in the bushes and thought
and thought, but he don't make no head nor tails of this kind
of business. Then he say to himself, says he:

"Well, if this don't beat everything!" says he. "Right down
there in that well Brer Rabbit keep his money hid, and if it ain't
that, he done gone and 'scovered a gold mine, and if it ain't
that, then I'm a-going to see what's in there," says he.

Brer Fox crope up a little nearer, he did, and listen, but he don't hear no fuss, and he keep on getting nearer, and yet he don't hear nothing. By and by he get up close and peep down, but he don't see nothing, and he don't hear nothing. All this time Brer Rabbit was mighty near scared out of his skin, and he feared for to move 'cause the bucket might keel over and spill him out in the water. While he saying his prayers over and over, old Brer Fox holler out:

"Heyo, Brer Rabbit! Who you visitin' down there?" says he.

"Who? Me? Oh, I'm just a-fishing, Brer Fox," says Brer Rabbit, says he. "I just say to myself that I'd sort of s'prise you all with a mess of fishes, and so here I is, and there's the fishes. I'm a-fishing for supper, Brer Fox," says Brer Rabbit, says he.

"Is there many of them down there, Brer Rabbit?" says Brer Fox, says he.

"Lots of them, Brer Fox; scores and scores of them. The water is naturally alive with them. Come down and help me haul them in, Brer Fox," says Brer Rabbit, says he.

"How I going to get down, Brer Rabbit?"

"Jump into the other bucket, Brer Fox. It'll fetch you down all safe and sound."

Brer Rabbit talked so happy and talked so sweet that Brer Fox he jump in the bucket, he did, and so he went down, 'cause his weight pulled Brer Rabbit up. When they pass one another on the half-way ground, Brer Rabbit he sing out:

> *"Good-bye, Brer Fox, take care o' your clothes,*
> *For this is the way the world goes;*
> *Some goes up and some goes down,*
> *You'll get to the bottom all safe and soun'."*

When Brer Rabbit got out, he gallop off and told the folks what the well belonged to, that Brer Fox was down there muddying up the drinking water, and then he gallop back to the well, and holler down to Brer Fox:

> *"Here come a man with a great big gun—*
> *When he haul you up, you jump and run."*

Well, soon enough Brer Fox was out of the well, and in just about half an hour both of them was back on the new ground working just as if they'd never heard of no well. But every now and then Brer Rabbit would burst out laughing, and old Brer Fox would scowl and say nothing.

Giacco and his Bean

—————————————◆—————————————

Giacco was all alone in the world. The only thing he had was a cupful of beans, and one of these he used to eat each day until finally there was only one left.

"I won't eat this bean," said Giacco. "I'll put it in my pocket and perhaps it will bring me good luck."

So he set out on his journeys, singing and whistling merrily to keep his spirits up, until he arrived at a quaint little house made of wood and china. He knocked at the door and a strange old man with a silver beard came and asked what he wanted.

"If you please, sir," said Giacco politely, "I have no father or mother and I have nothing to eat except this one bean which I keep hidden in my pocket to bring me luck."

"You poor lad," said the strange old man. He gave Giacco six walnuts to eat and let him sleep in his kitchen for the night. But during the night, Giacco's bean rolled out of his pocket and the strange old man's cat ate it up.

Giacco woke in the morning to find no bean in his pocket. He said to the old man, "Kind sir, my bean has disappeared from my pocket. Whatever shall I do?"

"My naughty cat must have eaten it up," said the old man. "He's a wicked animal. You may take him with you on your journeys."

Giacco thanked the old man and continued on his way with the wicked cat. Towards nightfall he arrived at a house made of paper and tin. He knocked at the door and a funny little woman came out and asked him what he wanted.

"I have no father or mother," replied Giacco. "I've only got this wicked cat that ate my good-luck bean."

"You poor thing," said the funny little woman. She gave him ten cherries to eat and let him sleep the night in her back-parlour. During the night the funny little woman's dog came and ate the cat and in the morning Giacco told her about it.

"That dog is a nasty brute. You can take it with you on your journeys," said the funny little woman.

So Giacco set off once more with the brute of a dog until towards evening he arrived at a house made of cardboard and feathers. When he knocked at the door, a bald-headed man came and asked him what he wanted.

"I've no father or mother," said Giacco, "only this brute of a dog that ate the cat that ate my good-luck bean."

"I'm very sorry to hear your bad news," said the bald-headed man. He gave Giacco three apples to eat and let him sleep the night in his pig-sty.

But during the night the pig ate the dog and in the morning Giacco told the bald-headed man that his dog had disappeared.

"It must have been that disgusting pig of mine. You can have him to accompany you on your journeys."

So Giacco continued his travels with the pig trotting behind him.

As it grew dark he came to a tiny house made of baskets and straw. He called out through a hole in the straw and a tall girl with long flaxen plaits came and asked him what he wanted.

"I have no father or mother," said Giacco, "only this pig that ate the dog that ate the cat that ate my good-luck bean."

"Sad," said the tall girl, "very sad." And she gave him a juicy peach to eat and let him sleep the night in the stable.

During the night the horse ate the pig and when Giacco awoke in the morning he cried out, "Hi! my pig has disappeared!"

"That must have been that silly horse of mine," said the

flaxen-plaited maiden. "I'll have nothing more to do with him Take him with you on your journeys."

So Giacco rode off on the horse and he travelled quite a long way until he arrived at a castle. He banged the big iron knocker on the gate and a great big soldier came to ask what he wanted.

"My name is Giacco," said the boy. "I have no father or mother. All I have in the world is this horse that ate the pig that ate the dog that ate the cat that ate my good-luck bean."

"Ha! Ha! Ha!" laughed the soldier, "Ha! Ha! Ha! Ha! Ha! Ha! Jolly good! Jolly good! I must go and tell the King."

"Ha! Ha! Ha! Ho! Ho! Ho!" laughed the King. "That's the

most comical story I have ever heard. Ha! Ha! Ha! Ho! Ho! Ho! Fancy a bean eating a dog that ate a horse that ate a pig! Ha! Ha! Ha! Ho! Ho! Ho!"

"If you will permit me to correct Your Majesty," said Giacco making a low bow, "it wasn't quite like that. It was the horse

that ate the pig that ate the dog that ate the cat that ate my
good-luck bean."

"My mistake," said the King, "ho! ho! You are quite right,
young man. It was the pig that ate the horse, no, I mean it was
the bean that ate the pig, no, it was . . ." and he went off again
into a great peal of laughter. And all the lords and ladies in the
court began to laugh and the cooks in the kitchens began to
laugh and the grooms in the stables and the soldiers outside in

the yard and then the people outside in the streets. . . . And soon the whole kingdom was roaring with laughter.

"Look here, Giacco," said the King when he had managed to get his breath. "If you tell me this story about your good-luck bean eating the dog, no, I mean about the pig eating the horse, no . . . well you know what I mean, young man. If you tell me that story every day, you can sit on a throne next to me and wear a golden crown and be treated just like me. Ha! Ha! Ha! Ho! Ho! Ho!"

And everybody burst into huge peals of laughter all over again, and Giacco lived happily ever after.

The Horse and the Lion

The lion was hungry. Hunting hadn't been too good during the past week. He was sitting by the roadside feeling sorry for himself when a handsome horse came trotting past. The lion's mouth watered as he thought what a wonderful dinner the horse would make if only he could catch him. The lion couldn't get his mind off that horse. So he let it be noised about that he had become a wonderful doctor who could heal any animal's complaint.

A day or two later the horse, pretending that he had a thorn in his hoof, came to the lion's den for help. The lion licked his chops. This was the chance he had been looking for. He asked the horse to raise one of his hind feet so that he could make an examination. Solicitously, in his best bedside manner, he bent his head as though to examine the ailing hoof. Just as the lion was ready to spring, the horse let go with his upraised hoof. There was a sickening thud as hoof met nose. And the last thing the lion remembered was a whinny of laughter as the horse galloped away towards the forest.

A Meal with a Magician

I have had some very odd meals in my time, and if I liked I could tell you about a meal in a mine, or a meal in Moscow, or a meal with a millionaire. But I think you will be more interested to hear about a meal I had one evening with a magician, because it is more unusual. People don't often have a meal of that sort, for rather few people know a magician at all well, because there aren't very many in England. Of course I am talking about real magicians. Some conjurors call themselves magicians, and they are very clever men. But they can't do the sort of things that real magicians do. I mean, a conjuror can turn a rabbit into a bowl of goldfish, but it's always done under cover or behind something, so that you can't see just what is happening. But a real magician can turn a cow into a grandfather clock with people looking on all the time. Only it is very much harder work, and no one could do it twice a day, and six days a week, like a conjuror does with rabbits.

When I first met Mr. Leakey I never guessed he was a magician. I met him like this. I was going across the Haymarket about five o'clock one afternoon. When I got to the refuge by a lamp-post in the middle I stopped, but a little man who had crossed so far with me went on. Then he saw a motor-bus going down the hill and jumped back, which is always a silly thing to do. He jumped right in front of a car, and if I hadn't grabbed his overcoat collar and pulled him back on to the refuge, I think the car would have knocked him down. For it was wet weather, and the road was very greasy, so it only skidded when the driver put the brakes on.

The little man was very grateful, but dreadfully frightened, so I gave him my arm across the street, and saw him back to his home, which was quite near. I won't tell you where it was, because if I did you might go there and bother him, and if he got really grumpy it might be very awkward indeed for you. I mean, he might make some of your ears as big as a cabbage-leaf, or turn your hair green, or exchange your right and left feet, or something like that. And then everyone who saw you would burst out laughing, and say, "Here comes wonky Willie, or lop-sided Lizzie," or whatever your name is.

"I can't bear modern traffic," he said, "the motor-buses make me so frightened. If it wasn't for my work in London I should like to live on a little island where there are no roads, or on the top of a mountain, or somewhere like that." The little man was sure I had saved his life, and insisted on my having dinner with him, so I said I would come to dinner on Wednesday week. I didn't notice anything specially odd about him then, except that his ears were rather large and that he had a little tuft of hair on the top of each of them, rather like the lynx at the zoo. I remember I thought if I had hair there I would shave it off. He told me that his name was Leakey, and that he lived on the first floor.

Well, on Wednesday week I went to dinner with him. I went upstairs in a block of flats and knocked at a quite ordinary door, and the little hall of the flat was quite ordinary too, but when I got inside it was one of the oddest rooms I have ever seen. Instead of wallpaper there were curtains round it, embroidered with pictures of people and animals. There was a picture of two men building a house, and another of a man with a dog and a cross-bow hunting rabbits. I know they were made of embroidery, because I touched them, but it must have been a very funny sort of embroidery, because the pictures were always changing. As long as you looked at them they stayed still, but if you looked away and back again they had altered. During dinner the builders had put a fresh storey on the house, the hunter had shot a bird with his cross-bow, and his dog had caught two rabbits.

The furniture was very funny, too. There was a bookcase made out of what looked like glass with the largest books in it that I ever saw, none of them less than a foot high, and bound in leather. There were cupboards running along the tops of the bookshelves. The chairs were beautifully carved, with high wooden backs, and there were two tables. One was made of copper, and had a huge crystal globe on it. The other was a solid lump of wood about ten feet long, four feet wide, and three feet high, with holes cut in it so that you could get your knees under it. There were various odd things hanging from the ceiling. At first I couldn't make out how the room was lit. Then I saw that the light came from plants of a sort I had never seen before, growing in pots. They had red, yellow and blue fruits as big as tomatoes, which shone. They weren't disguised electric lamps, for I touched one and it was quite cold and soft like a fruit.

"Well," said Mr. Leakey, "what would you like for dinner?"

"Oh, whatever you've got," I said.

"You can have whatever you like," he said. "Please choose a soup."

So I thought he probably got his dinner from a restaurant, and I said, "I'll have a Bortsch," which is a red Russian soup with cream in it.

"Right," he said, "I'll get it ready. Look here, do you mind if we have dinner served the way mine usually is? You aren't easily frightened, are you?"

"Not very easily," I said.

"All right, then, I'll call my servant, but I warn you he's rather odd."

At that Mr. Leakey flapped the tops and lobes of his ears against his head. It made a noise like when one claps one's hands, but not so loud. Out of a large copper pot about as big as the copper you wash clothes in, which was standing in one corner, came what at first I thought was a large wet snake. Then I saw it had suckers all down one side, and was really the arm of an octopus. This arm opened a cupboard and pulled out a large towel with which it wiped the next arm that came out. The dry arm then clung on to the wall with its suckers, and gradually the whole beast came out, dried itself, and crawled up the wall. It was the largest octopus I have ever seen; each arm was about eight feet long, and its body was as big as a sack. It crawled up the wall, and then along the ceiling, holding on by its suckers like a fly. When it got above the table it held on by one arm only, and with the other seven got plates and

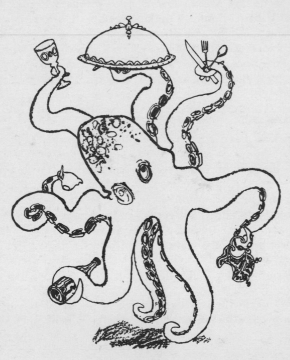

knives and forks out of the cupboards above the bookshelves and laid the table with them.

"That's my servant Oliver," said Mr. Leakey. "He's much better than a person, because he has more arms to work with, and he can hold on to a plate with about ten suckers, so he never drops one."

When Oliver the octopus had laid the table we sat down and he offered me a choice of water, lemonade, beer, and four different kinds of wine with his seven free arms, each of which held a different bottle. I chose some water and some very good wine from Burgundy.

All this was so odd that I was not surprised to notice that my host was wearing a top hat, but I certainly did think it a little queer when he took it off and poured two platefuls of soup out of it.

"Ah, we want some cream," he added. "Come here, Phyllis." At this a small green cow, about the size of a rabbit, ran out of a hutch, jumped on to the table, and stood in front of Mr. Leakey, who milked her into a silver cream jug which Oliver had handed down for the purpose. The cream was excellent, and I enjoyed the soup very much.

"What would you like next?" said Mr. Leakey.

"I leave it to you," I answered.

"All right," he said, "we'll have grilled turbot, and turkey to follow. Catch us a turbot, please, Oliver, and be ready to grill it, Pompey."

At this Oliver picked up a fish-hook with the end of one of his arms and began making casts in the air like a fly-fisher. Meanwhile I heard a noise in the fireplace, and Pompey came out. He was a small dragon about a foot long, not counting his tail, which measured another foot. He had been lying on the burning coals, and was red-hot. So I was glad to see that as soon as he got out of the fire he put a pair of asbestos boots which were lying in the fender on to his hind feet.

"Now, Pompey," said Mr. Leakey, "hold your tail up properly. If you burn the carpet again, I'll pour a bucket of cold water over you. (Of course, I wouldn't really do that; it's very cruel to pour cold water on a dragon, especially a little one with a thin skin)," he added in a low voice, which only I could hear. But poor Pompey took the threat quite seriously. He whimpered, and the yellow flames which were coming out of his nose turned a dull blue. He waddled along rather clumsily on his hind legs, holding up his tail and the front part of his body. I think the asbestos boots made walking rather difficult for him, though they saved the carpet, and no doubt kept his hind feet warm. But of course dragons generally walk on all four feet and seldom wear boots, so I was surprised that Pompey walked as well as he did.

I was so busy watching Pompey that I never saw how Oliver caught the turbot, and by the time I looked up at him again he had just finished cleaning it, and threw it down to Pompey. Pompey caught it in his front paws, which had cooled down a bit, and were just about the right temperature for grilling things. He had long thin fingers with claws on the end; and held the fish on each hand alternately, holding the other against his red-hot chest to warm it. By the time he had finished and put the grilled fish on to a plate which Oliver handed down, Pompey was clearly feeling the cold, for his teeth were chattering, and he scampered back to the fire with evident joy.

"Yes," said Mr. Leakey, "I know some people say it is cruel to let a young dragon cool down like that, and liable to give it a bad cold. But I say a dragon can't begin to learn too soon that life isn't all fire and flames, and the world is a colder place than he'd like it to be. And they don't get colds if you give them plenty of sulphur to eat. Of course a dragon with a cold is an awful nuisance to itself and everyone else. I've known one throw flames for a hundred yards when it sneezed. But that was a full-grown one, of course. It burned down one of the Emperor of China's palaces. Besides, I really couldn't afford to keep a dragon if I didn't make use of him. Last week, for example, I used his breath to burn the old paint off the door, and his tail makes quite a good soldering iron. Then he's really much more reliable than a dog for dealing with burglars. They might shoot a dog, but leaden bullets just melt the moment they touch Pompey. Anyway, I think dragons were meant for use, not ornament. Don't you?"

"Well, do you know," I answered, "I am ashamed to say that Pompey is the first live dragon I've ever seen."

"Of course," said Mr. Leakey, "how stupid of me. I have so few guests here except professional colleagues that I forgot you were a layman. By the way," he went on, as he poured sauce out of his hat over the fish, "I don't know if you've noticed anything queer about this dinner. Of course some people are more observant than others."

"Well," I answered, "I've never seen anything like it before."

For example at that moment I was admiring an enormous

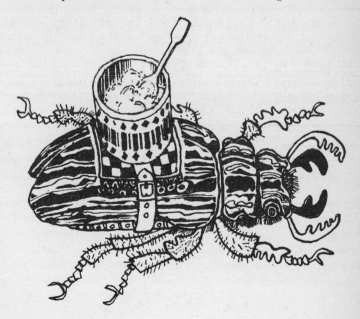

rainbow-coloured beetle which was crawling towards me over the table with a salt-cellar strapped on its back.

"Ah well then," said my host, "perhaps you have guessed that I'm a magician. Pompey, of course, is a real dragon, but most of the other animals here were people before I made them what they are now. Take Oliver, for example. When he was a man he had his legs cut off by a railway train. I couldn't stick them on again because my magic doesn't work against machinery. Poor Oliver was bleeding to death, so I thought the only way to save his life was to turn him into some animal with no legs. Then he couldn't have any legs to have been cut off. I turned him into a snail, and took him home in my pocket. But whenever I tried to turn him back into something more interesting, like a dog, it had no hind legs. But an octopus has really got no legs. Those eight tentacles grow out of its head. So when I turned him into an octopus, he was all right. And he had been a waiter when he was a man, so he soon learnt his job. I think he's much better than a maid because he can lift the plates from above, and doesn't stand behind one and breathe down one's neck. You may have the rest of the fish, Oliver, and a bottle of beer. I know that's what you like."

Oliver seized the fish in one of his arms and put it into an immense beak like a parrot's but much bigger, which lay in the centre of the eight arms. Then he took a bottle of beer out of a cupboard, unscrewed the cork with his beak, hoisted himself up to the ceiling with two of his other arms, and turned over so that his mouth was upwards. As he emptied the bottle he winked one of his enormous eyes. Then I felt sure he must be really a man, for I never saw an ordinary octopus wink.

The turkey came in a more ordinary way. Oliver let down a large hot plate, and then a dish-cover on to it. There was nothing in the cover, as I could see. Mr. Leakey got up, took a large wand out of the umbrella stand, pointed it at the dish-cover, said a few words, and there was the turkey steaming hot when Oliver lifted the cover off it.

A Meal with a Magician

"Of course that's easy," said Mr. Leakey, "any good conjuror could do it, but you can never be sure the food you get in that way is absolutely fresh. That's why I like to see my fish caught. But birds are all the better for being a few days old. Ah, we shall want some sausages too. That's easy."

He took a small clay pipe out of his pocket and blew into it. A large brown bubble came out of the other end, shaped like a sausage. Oliver picked it off with the end of one of his tentacles, and put it on a hot plate, and it was a sausage, because I ate it. He made six sausages in this way, and while I was watching him Oliver had handed down the vegetables. I don't know where he got them. The sauce and gravy came out of Mr. Leakey's hat, as usual.

Just after this the only accident of the evening happened. The beetle who carried the salt-cellar round tripped over a fold in the tablecloth and spilled the salt just in front of Mr. Leakey, who spoke to him very angrily.

"It's lucky for you, Leopold, that I'm a sensible man. If I were superstitious, which I'm not, I should think I was going to have bad luck. But it's you who are going to have bad luck, if anyone. I've a good mind to turn you back into a man, and if I do, I'll put you straight on to that carpet and send you to the nearest police station; and when the police ask you where you've been hiding, d'you think they'll believe you when you say you've been a beetle for the last year? Are you sorry?"

Leopold, with a great struggle, got out of his harness and rolled on to his back, feebly waving his legs in the air like a dog does when he's ashamed of himself.

"When Leopold was a man," said Mr. Leakey, "he made money by swindling people. When the police found it out and were going to arrest him, he came to me for help, but I thought it served him right. So I said 'If they catch you, you'll get sent to penal servitude for seven years. If you like I'll turn you into a beetle for five years, which isn't so long, and then, if you've been a good beetle, I'll make you into a man with a different sort of face, so the police won't know you.' So now Leopold is a beetle. Well, I see he's sorry for spilling the salt. Now, Leopold, you must pick up all the salt you've spilt.''

He turned Leopold over on his front and I watched him begin to pick the salt up. It took him over an hour. First he picked it up a grain at a time in his mouth, lifted himself on his front legs, and dropped it into the salt-cellar. Then he thought of a better plan. He was a beetle of the kind whose feelers are short and spread out into a fan. He started shovelling the salt with his feelers, and got on much quicker that way. But fairly soon he got uncomfortable. His feelers started to itch or something, and he had to wipe them with his legs. Finally he got a bit of paper and used it for a shovel, holding it with his front feet.

"That's very clever for a beetle," said my host. "When I turn him back into a man he'll be quite good with his hands, and I expect he'll be able to earn his living at an honest job."

As we were finishing the turkey, Mr. Leakey looked up anxiously from time to time.

"I hope Abdu'l Makkar won't be late with the strawberries," he said.

"Strawberries?" I asked in amazement, for it was the middle of January.

"Oh yes, I've sent Abdu'l Makkar, who is a jinn, to New Zealand for some. Of course it's summer there. He oughtn't to be long now, if he has been good, but you know what jinns are, they have their faults, like the rest of us. Curiosity, especially. When one sends them on long errands they will fly too high. They like to get quite close to Heaven to overhear what the angels are saying, and then the angels throw shooting stars at them. Then they drop their parcels, or come home half-scorched. He ought to be back soon, he's been away over an hour. Meanwhile we'll have some other fruit, in case he's late."

He got up, and tapped the four corners of the table with his wand. At each corner the wood swelled; then it cracked, and a little green shoot came out and started growing. In a minute they were already about a foot high, with several leaves at the top, and the bottom quite woody. I could see from the leaves that one was a cherry, another a pear, and the third a peach, but I didn't know the fourth.

As Oliver was clearing away the remains of the turkey with four of his arms and helping himself to a sausage with a fifth, Abdu'l Makkar came in. He came feet first through the ceiling, which seemed to close behind him like water in the tank of the diving birds' house in the Zoo, when you look at it from underneath while a penguin dives in. It shook a little for a moment afterwards. He narrowly missed one of Oliver's arms, but alighted safely on the floor, bending his knees to break his fall, and bowing deeply to Mr. Leakey. He had a brown face with rather a long nose, and looked like a man, except that he had a pair of leathery wings folded on his back, and his nails were of gold. He wore a turban and clothes of green silk.

"O peacock of the world and redresser of injustices," he said, "thy unworthy servant comes into the presence with rare and refreshing fruit."

"The presence deigns to express gratification at the result of thy labours."

"The joy of thy negligible slave is as the joy of King Solomon, son of David (on whom be peace, if he has not already obtained peace) when he first beheld Balkis, the queen of Sheba. May the Terminator of delights and Separator of companions be far from this dwelling."

"May the Deluder of Intelligence never trouble the profundity of thine apprehension."

"O dominator of demons and governor of goblins, what egregious enchanter or noble necromancer graces thy board?"

"It is written, O Abdu'l Makkar, in the book of the sayings of the prophet Shoaib, the apostle of the Midianites, that curiosity slew the cat of Pharaoh, king of Egypt."

"That is a true word."

"Thy departure is permitted. Awaken me at the accustomed

139

hour. But stay! My safety razor hath no more blades and the shops of London are closed. Fly therefore to Montreal, where it is even now high noon, and purchase me a packet thereof."

"I tremble and obey."

"Why dost thou tremble, O audacious among the Ifreets?"

"O Emperor of enchantment, the lower air is full of aeroplanes, flying swifter than a magic carpet, and each making a din like unto the bursting of the great dam of Sheba, and the upper air is infested with meteorites."

"Fly therefore at a height of five miles and thou shalt avoid both the one peril and the other. And now, O performer of commands and executor of behests, thou hast my leave to depart."

"May the wisdom of Plato, the longevity of Shiqq, the wealth of Solomon, and the success of Alexander, be thine."

"The like unto thee, with brazen knobs thereon."

The jinn now vanished, this time through the floor. While he and Mr. Leakey had been talking the trees had grown up to about four feet high, and flowered. The flowers were now falling off, and little green fruits were swelling.

"You have to talk like that to a jinn or you lose his respect. I hope you don't mind my not introducing you, but really jinns may be quite awkward at times," said my host. "Of course Abdu'l Makkar is a nice chap and means well, but he might be very embarrassing to you, as you don't know the Word of Power to send him away. For instance if you were playing cricket and went in against a fast bowler, he'd probably turn up and ask you 'Shall I slay thine enemy, O Defender of Stumps, or merely convert him into an he-goat of loathsome appearance and afflicted with the mange?' You know I used to be very fond of watching cricket, but I can't do it now. Quite a little magic will upset a match. Last year I went to see the Australians playing against Gloucester, and just because I felt a little sympathetic with Gloucestershire the Australian wickets went down like ninepins. If I hadn't left before the end they'd have been beaten. And after that I couldn't go to any of the test matches. After all, one wants the best side to win."

We next ate the New Zealand strawberries, which were very good, with Phyllis's cream. While we did so Pompey, who acted as a sort of walking stove, came out again and melted some cheese to make a Welsh rarebit. After this we went on to dessert. The fruit was now quite ripe. The fourth tree bore half a dozen golden fruits shaped rather like apricots, but much bigger, and my host told me they were mangoes, which of course usually grow in India. In fact you can't make them grow in England except by magic. So I said I would try a mango.

"Aha," said Mr. Leakey, "this is where I have a pull over Lord Melchett or the Duke of Westminster, or any other rich man. They might be able to get mangoes here by aeroplane, but they couldn't give them as dessert at a smart dinner-party."

"Why not?" I asked.

"That shows you've never eaten one. The only proper place to eat a mango is in your bath. You see, it has a tough skin and a squashy inside, so when once you get through the skin all the juice squirts out. And that would make a nasty mess of people's white shirts. D'you ever wear a stiff-fronted shirt?"

"Not often."

"A good thing too. You probably don't know why people wear them. It's a curious story. About a hundred years ago a great Mexican enchanter called Whiztopacoatl came over to Europe. And he got very annoyed with the rich men. He didn't so much mind their being rich, but he thought they spent their money on such ugly things, and were dreadfully stodgy and smug. So he decided to turn them all into turtles. Now to do that somebody has to say two different spells at the same time, which is pretty difficult, I can tell you. So Whiztopacoatl went round to an English sorcerer called Mr. Benedict Barnacle, to borrow a two-headed parrot that belonged to him. It was rather like one of those two-headed eagles they used to have on the Russian and Austrian flags. Then he was going to teach one of the heads one spell, and the other head the second spell; and when the parrot said both at once all the rich men would have turned into turtles. But Mr. Barnacle persuaded him to be less fierce, so finally they agreed that for a hundred years the rich men in Europe should be made to wear clothes only fit for turtles. Because of course the front of the turtle is stiff and flat, and it is the only sort of animal that would be quite comfortable in a shirt with a stiff flat front. They made a spell to stiffen all the shirts, and of course it worked very well, but it's wearing off now, and soon nobody will wear such silly clothes any more.

"About your mango; you can eat it quite safely, if you just wait a moment while I enchant it so that it won't splash over you."

Quite a short spell and a little wiggling of his wand were enough, and then I ate a mango. It was wonderful. It was the only fruit I have ever eaten that was better than the best strawberries. I can't describe the flavour, which is a mixture of all sorts of things, including a little resin, like the smell of a pine forest in summer. There is a huge flattish stone in the middle, too big to get into your mouth, and all round it a squashy yellow pulp. To test the spell I tried to spill some down my waistcoat, but it merely jumped up into my mouth. Mr. Leakey ate a pear, and gave me the other five mangoes to take home. But I had to eat them in my bath because they weren't enchanted.

While we were having coffee (out of the hat, of course) Mr. Leakey rubbed one corner of the table with his wand and it began to sprout with very fine grass. When it was about as high as the grass on a lawn, he called Phyllis out of her hutch, and she ate some of it for her dinner. We talked for a while about magic, football, and the odder sorts of dog, such as Bedlington terriers and rough-haired Dachshunds, and then I said I must be getting home.

"I'll take you home," said Mr. Leakey, "but when you have a day to spare you must come round and spend it with me, if you'd care to see the sort of things I generally do, and we might go over to India or Java or somewhere for the afternoon. Let me know when you're free. But now just stand on this carpet, and shut your eyes, because people often get giddy the first two or three times they travel by magic carpet."

We got on to the carpet. I took a last look at the table, where Leopold had just finished picking up the salt, and was resting, while Phyllis was chewing the cud. Then I shut my eyes, my host told the carpet my address, flapped his ears, and I felt a rush of cold air on my cheeks, and a slight giddiness. Then the air was warm again. Mr. Leakey told me to open my eyes, and I was in my sitting-room at home, five miles away. As the room is small, and there were a number of books and things on the floor, the carpet could not settle down properly, and stayed about a foot up in the air. Luckily it was quite stiff, so I stepped down off it, and turned the light on.

"Good-night," said Mr. Leakey, bending down to shake my hand, and then he flapped his ears and he and the carpet vanished. I was left in my room with nothing but a nice full feeling and a parcel of mangoes to persuade me that I had not been dreaming.

The Elephant's Picnic

Elephants are generally clever animals, but there was once an elephant who was very silly; and his great friend was a kangaroo. Now, kangaroos are not often clever animals, and this one certainly was not, so she and the elephant got on very well together.

One day they thought they would like to go off for a picnic by themselves. But they did not know anything about picnics, and had not the faintest idea of what to do to get ready.

"What do you do on a picnic?" the elephant asked a child he knew.

"Oh, we collect wood and make a fire, and then we boil the kettle," said the child.

"What do you boil the kettle for?" said the elephant in surprise.

"Why, for tea, of course," said the child in a snapping sort of way; so the elephant did not like to ask any more questions. But he went and told the kangaroo, and they collected together all the things they thought they would need.

When they got to the place where they were going to have their picnic, the kangaroo said that she would collect the wood because she had got a pouch to carry it back in. A kangaroo's pouch, of course, is very small; so the kangaroo carefully chose the smallest twigs she could find, and only about five or six of those. In fact, it took a lot of hopping to find any sticks small enough to go in her pouch at all; and it was a long time before she came back. But silly though the elephant was, he soon saw those sticks would not be enough for a fire.

"Now I will go off and get some wood," he said.

His ideas of getting wood were different. Instead of taking little twigs he pushed down whole trees with his forehead, and staggered back to the picnic-place with them rolled up in his trunk. Then the kangaroo struck a match, and they lit a bonfire made of whole trees. The blaze, of course, was enormous, and the fire was so hot that for a long time they could not get near it; and it was not until it began to die down a bit that they were able to get near enough to cook anything.

"Now let's boil the kettle," said the elephant. Amongst the things he had brought was a brightly shining copper kettle and a very large black iron saucepan. The elephant filled the saucepan with water.

"What are you doing that for?" said the kangaroo.

"To boil the kettle in, you silly," said the elephant. So he popped the kettle in the saucepan of water, and put the saucepan on the fire; for he thought, the old juggins, that you boil a kettle in the same way you boil an egg, or boil a cabbage! And the kangaroo, of course, did not know any better.

So they boiled and boiled the kettle, and every now and then they prodded it with a stick.

"It doesn't seem to be getting tender," said the elephant sadly, "and I'm sure we can't eat it for tea until it does."

So then away he went and got more wood for the fire; and still the saucepan boiled and boiled, and still the kettle remained as hard as ever. It was getting late now, almost dark.

"I'm afraid it won't be ready for tea," said the kangaroo. "I am afraid we shall have to spend the night here. I wish we had got something with us to sleep in."

"Haven't you?" said the elephant. "You mean to say you didn't pack before you came away?"

"No," said the kangaroo. "What should I have packed anyway?"

145

"Why, your trunk, of course," said the elephant. "That is what people pack."

"But I haven't got a trunk," said the kangaroo.

"Well, I have," said the elephant, "and I've packed it! Kindly pass the pepper; I want to unpack!"

So then the kangaroo passed the elephant the pepper, and the elephant took a good sniff. Then he gave a most tremendous sneeze, and everything he had packed in his trunk shot out of it—tooth-brush, spare socks, gym shoes, a comb, a bag of bull's-eyes, his pyjamas, and his Sunday suit. So then the elephant put on his pyjamas and lay down to sleep; but the kangaroo had no pyjamas, and so, of course, she could not sleep.

"All right," she said to the elephant; "you sleep; and I will sit up and keep the fire going."

So all night the kangaroo kept the fire blazing brightly and the kettle boiling merrily in the saucepan. When the next morning came the elephant woke up.

"Now," he said, "let's have our breakfast."

So they took the kettle out of the saucepan; and what do you think? It was boiled as tender as tender could be! So they cut it fairly in half and shared it between them, and ate it for breakfast; and both agreed they had never had so good a breakfast in their lives.

The Language of Animals

❖

In the heart of Serbia lies a dark forest. Now this forest is enchanted, although the people who live round there don't know it.

One day a poor shepherd was driving his sheep along a path when he heard a peculiar hissing sound. As he came nearer he noticed a clump of bushes on fire and there, trapped in the flames, was a snake hissing and crying for help. The shepherd was a kind man and he could not but feel sorry for this poisonous reptile. But imagine his surprise when the snake addressed him in his own language. "O Shepherd, do save me from this fire, I beseech you." Quickly the shepherd stretched out his crook and the snake entwined itself around the stick. But to his horror, as soon as it was safe, the serpent uncoiled itself from the stick and crept around his arm and shoulders till he felt it almost throttling his neck. Trembling with fear the poor shepherd cried, "Ungrateful wretch, are you going to kill me when I have saved your life?"

"Have no fear, my saviour," hissed the snake gently, "just take me to my father's house; he is the snake king and will richly reward you for what you have done." The shepherd was terrified at the thought of meeting the snake king and he tried to refuse, but the snake prince persuaded him, saying nothing would happen to his sheep while he was away, and he would never regret his visit. So the poor man left his sheep and crossed the enchanted forest with the snake still twisted round his neck,

till they came to a fine palace built of golden beech leaves, with
a gateway made of living serpents coiling and writhing about in
fantastic patterns. But the snake prince hissed at them and they
all untwined, so that the shepherd could pass in peace. Then
the snake prince said to him, "My father will offer you riches,
gold, silver, precious stones—anything you wish. But don't be
tempted by these; instead ask him to grant you the gift of
understanding the language of animals. He may refuse you at

148

first but in the end he will have to grant your request."

They found the king, coiled, fast asleep on his throne of polished stone. His skin was shrivelled with age and on his crest he wore a crown of gold. Great was his joy when he awoke to find his beloved son beside him. When the snake prince told him how his life had been saved the king turned to the shepherd and asked him to name his own reward. The shepherd approached the throne fearfully and said timidly, "My only wish is to be given the language of animals." At this the king shook his head dolefully and answered:

"All my riches are at your disposal but I cannot grant your request. It is too dangerous for mere humans, for if ever they reveal their secret power they are doomed to instant death." But the shepherd persisted in his demand until, seeing that the king would not give in, he turned to go.

But the king stopped him, saying, "Oh you who have saved my son, seeing you are determined to have this wish and no other, I shall no longer refuse you. Open your mouth."

The shepherd obeyed and the king blew three times into his mouth with a fiery breath. Then the king bade him blow back into his mouth. This the shepherd did and the king said, "Now the language of animals is yours, but remember, never share your secret with anyone or you will die instantly. Farewell."

The shepherd left the snake palace and as he returned through the enchanted forest he found he could understand every word that passed between birds, rabbits, squirrels, foxes and all the other creatures.

At last he came to the glade where he had left his flock and in wonderment found that they were all there. He was just settling down to rest on the soft moss when two ravens alighted on a nearby tree and began to gossip. Said one of them, "If this man only knew that under the moss where he is resting lies a cave full of silver and gold, he would hurry off to get himself a cart and spade." At this the shepherd leapt up, gathered his flock and hurried home to tell his master, a wealthy farmer.

The farmer was an honest, generous man and though he helped the shepherd dig until they came to a cave brimful of gold and silver coins, he refused to accept a single piece, saying, "It was you that God gave it to. Build yourself a house, marry and start your own farm and may fortune bless you."

The shepherd followed his master's advice and so well did his farm flourish that he soon became the richest man in the district. He was so rich in fact that the local squire was glad to accept him as a son-in-law. His young wife was beautiful, but very headstrong. At first the simple shepherd was too impressed by her superior education to notice her faults. Although he was now a wealthy man, he never forgot his humble origin and one day before Christmas he told his wife: "Make ready enough food and wine for a hundred men. Tomorrow we will go to our farm and feast the servants while I myself guard the sheep."

So one bitter winter night when the snow lay thick on the ground the kind man went to watch over the sheep while his shepherds feasted and made merry round a roaring fire. Just before midnight the wolves began to howl and the dogs to growl. Then the shepherd heard the leader of the wolf pack asking the dogs in their own tongue: "Can we come and kill the sheep, and then we can all feast on them together?" To this the dogs answered, "With pleasure, for we are sick of guarding other people's property." Only one old dog, with but two fangs left in his head, snarled at them; "The devil take you: as long as I have these two fangs left, you shall not touch my master's sheep."

Next morning the shepherd ordered his servants to kill all his dogs except the one faithful old hound. The servants pleaded with him, saying that he was surely mad to kill a whole pack of well-trained sheepdogs. But their master insisted that they carry out his orders. Then he mounted a piebald horse and his wife rode on a grey mare, and they set off for home. Soon the mare began to lag behind, whereupon the horse neighed, "Hurry up! Why do you dawdle?" To which the mare replied,

"It is easy for you to say 'Hurry'. You have only the master on your back but I carry the mistress, whose rules are a burden to the whole household." Hearing these words, the shepherd burst into such a hearty laugh that his wife spurred on her mare to ask him the cause of his mirth.

He was unable to explain and this only made her the more inquisitive, till at last, worn out by her obstinate questioning, he tried to excuse himself by saying, "Don't keep asking me, for if I tell you the reason I shall die forthwith."

But his wife was a stubborn creature, and thought he was joking again, and continued to press him for an answer, until, poor man, he could stand it no longer, being quite unable to withstand her nagging. So when he reached home he sadly ordered a coffin to be made and placed in the courtyard. Then he stepped into it and told his wife, "I'm going to lie in this coffin, for I shall die as soon as I tell you why I laughed."

But before lying down in the coffin he turned to take one last look at his beloved fields, and he saw his faithful old dog come running towards him. Seeing what was about to become of his master, the poor hound began to howl woefully and refused to touch the delicious cakes his mistress offered him. The cock, however, came strutting in from the yard, eager to seize any morsel that happened to be lying about. The dog began to rebuke him for his heartlessness, saying: "You greedy creature, how can you think of nothing but food when our poor master is about to die?" But the cock only tossed his crimson comb and answered, "What do I care if such a fool is about to die! Why, I have a hundred wives and I gather them all around a grain of corn, only to gobble it up myself when they are all assembled. And if any of them dares to protest I just peck them. But he, the fool, cannot control his one and only spouse."

Hearing this the shepherd leaped from the coffin, seized a stick and called to his wife: "Just listen, my good woman. If you still insist on knowing why I laughed, I shall beat the living daylights out of you."

Needless to say his wife instantly stopped her nagging and what's more, she never nagged again and they lived happily ever after.

The Wicked Little Jackal

Africa, as you probably know, is always a very hot country, but the year when this story took place it was *exceptionally* hot. There was no rain, all the rivers and pools dried up, the grass withered and the trees died. The animals went around with their tongues hanging out, dying of thirst, waiting and waiting for the rain to fall.

At long last it did fall. The grass grew green once more, the trees stood up straight and the animals quenched their thirst in the newly-filled pools and rivers.

A meeting of all the animals was called to decide what to do if another terrible drought were to come. After a lot of discussion they all agreed that the best plan was to dig a very large, very deep hole near a spring so that the water could trickle into it and build up into a great pool. Then they wouldn't have to worry if no rain fell, because there would always be water in the pool.

"Who is going to dig this hole?" asked the elephant.

"You, my friend," replied the lion, who, as king of the forest, was in charge of the meeting. "And you, and you, and you, and you, and you," the lion continued, pointing to each animal in turn. "We are *all* going to dig this hole, because we shall *all* be drinking the water in it. I, of course, will supervise the proceedings."

He paused and looked round sternly. "I take it that you all agree to do a share of the digging." The animals said "Oh yes,

Your Majesty, we all agree to do our share of the digging."

So they went and found a spring and not far from it they all began to dig. Did I say 'all'? Well, not exactly all, because the jackal did not join in. Now everybody knew the jackal was mean and greedy and always stealing other people's food instead of hunting for his own. Oh yes, they all knew Brother Jackal very well. But they did expect him to help with the digging.

"Come on, Jackal," they all urged, "come and give a hand. You'll be using this water as well, you know."

But the jackal just sat and laughed. "Work?" he said. "Not likely. You work and I will enjoy the water when you have finished."

The animals were very angry but they knew it was not much use arguing with the cunning little jackal, so they went on working while the jackal just sat and laughed.

At long last the pool was finished and the beautiful, fresh spring water began to flow into it.

"And now," said the lion, "we must build a high wall round it, just leaving room enough for a narrow gate. And then we will appoint a guard to watch over it so that the jackal won't be able to come and steal the water from the pool which we have all worked so hard to build. I am determined to see that he shall not enjoy the fruits of our labours."

So they built the wall and made a strong little gate.

"Now," said the lion, "who will volunteer to guard the gate?"

"I will, Your Majesty, I will," cried the hare.

"Excellent," said the lion. "I think Hare will make a very good guard—he has first-class eyesight, he can see in the dark and he is, of course, one of the fastest creatures in the whole animal kingdom."

That night, as the hare sat and watched, the jackal came strolling past, nibbling a piece of honeycomb. The cunning thing pretended not to see the hare (though, of course, he *had* seen him) and walked past again, still nibbling. "Delicious honey, this," he remarked, as though talking to himself. "So sweet, so succulent!" The hare felt very tempted. "Is it really so very tasty?" he asked. The jackal pretended not to hear but continued to nibble and say the most tantalising things. The hare asked once more: "Is the honeycomb really so wonderfully succulent?"

"Oh is that you, Hare?" asked the cunning jackal. "I hadn't noticed you in the dark. Yes, indeed. It's the most wonderful honeycomb I have ever tasted, and I'm quite an expert in these matters. Of course, I would gladly let you have a taste of it but all those angry animals would come and attack me if I dared come near you. You are supposed to be guarding this water, I understand."

"I promise you won't come to any harm," said the hare.

"Well, just to be on the safe side," said the jackal, "let me tie your paws and I'll put some honey into your mouth."

The hare agreed, for he thought that the jackal didn't really want any water. So the jackal tied the hare's paws, then jumped right over him, splash! into the cool, clear pool. He drank and drank to his heart's content. Then he stirred up the mud at the bottom of the pool to make it look as messy as possible and ran off without giving the hare any taste of the honey at all.

You can imagine how cross the animals were when they found their beautiful pool, at which they had worked so hard, all muddy and dirty. They started arguing and quarrelling among themselves about who should be the next to keep guard over the pool. And poor old Hare felt very foolish, sitting there with his paws tied up.

At last, when there was a lull in all the squabbling, the tortoise spoke up. "I will guard the water," she said. They were all taken aback for a moment, the tortoise being usually such a quiet creature, but eventually they agreed.

So that night the tortoise, with her head tucked into her shell and her feet and tail well drawn in, sat by the gate and waited.

Presently the jackal came along, nibbling at his honeycomb and chatting to himself.

"How would you like to taste some of my delicious honey?" he asked the tortoise. But the tortoise kept perfectly still and made no reply whatsoever.

The jackal tried again. "It's the most delicious honey in the whole world. Do have some."

But the tortoise remained perfectly motionless. The jackal took a closer look but he couldn't seem to make up his mind which was the tail and which was the head.

"She must be asleep," he muttered. "I'll go and help myself to a drink in the pool." And he was just about to step over the tortoise when crack! out popped the tortoise's little head and she caught the jackal by the hind leg. The jackal screeched and kicked and howled but the tortoise would not let go. He offered to give her all his honey and to get her any juicy green leaves she might fancy, but the tortoise held on and would not let go.

At last, with the first rays of dawn, the animals came along to see how everything had been going on and to have a drink in their pool.

When they saw the jackal trapped by his leg in the tortoise's mouth, they thought it such a comical sight that they roared with laughter. The jackal simply hated being laughed at and he felt most embarrassed at being found in that humiliating position. He was, after all, supposed to be a most cunning animal. As they all sat there, quite helpless with laughter, he just couldn't bear it any longer and gave one last desperate kick. The tortoise, feeling a bit sorry for him, let go, and the jackal ran away as fast as his legs could carry him. He ran and ran and ran. And never, ever again did he come back to spoil the animals' beautiful pool.

And all the animals were very grateful to the tortoise and treated her with great honour.

Puss and Pup

◆

Once upon a time Puss and Pup kept house together. They had their own little cottage in the wood. Here they lived together and tried to do everything just like real grown-up people. But somehow they couldn't always manage this. You see, they had small clumsy paws, without any fingers like people have, only little soft pads with claws on them. So they couldn't do everything just like real grown-ups. And they didn't go to school, because school is not meant for animals.

Of course it isn't. School is only for children.

Their home was not always as tidy as it might have been. Some things they did well, and others not so well. And sometimes there was rather a mess.

One day they noticed that the cottage floor was very dirty.

"I say, Pup," said Puss, "our floor's horribly dirty. Don't you think so?"

"Yes, I do. It really is rather dirty," said Pup. "Just look how grubby it's made my paws."

"They're filthy," said Puss. "Ugh, you ought to be ashamed of yourself! We must scrub the floor. People don't have dirty floors. They scrub them."

"All right," replied Pup. "But how are we going to do it?"

"Oh, it's easy," said Puss. "You go and fetch some water, and I'll see to the rest."

Pup took a pail and went for water. Meanwhile Puss took a piece of soap out of her bag and put it on the table. Then she went off to the box-room for something; I expect she kept a piece of smoked mouse there.

While she was away Pup came back with the water and saw something lying on the table. He unwrapped it. It was pink.

"Ha, ha! This looks good," said Pup to himself. And because it made him feel hungry, he pushed the whole piece into his mouth and started chewing it.

But it didn't taste so good. Soon Puss came in and heard Pup making all sorts of funny spluttering noises. She saw that Pup's mouth was full of foam and his eyes were streaming with tears.

"Goodness me!" cried Puss. "Whatever's happened to you, Pup? You must be ill. There's foam dripping from your mouth. Whatever's the matter?"

"Well," said Pup, "I found something lying on the table. I thought it might be some cheese, or a piece of cake, so I ate it. But it stings horribly and makes my mouth all full of foam."

"What a silly you are!" scolded Puss. "That was soap! Soap's for washing with, not eating."

"Oh," said Pup. "So that's why it hurts so much. Ow, ow, it stings, ow, it stings!"

"Have a good drink of water," suggested Puss; "that'll stop it smarting."

Pup drank away until he had finished up all the water. His mouth had stopped smarting by now, but there was still plenty of foam. So he went and wiped his muzzle on the grass outside. Then he had to go and fetch some more water because he had drunk it all and there was none left. Luckily Puss had some money, and she went off to buy some more soap.

"I won't eat that again," said Pup, when Puss returned with the soap. "But, Puss, how are we going to manage without a scrubbing brush?"

"I've already thought about that," said Puss. "You've got a rough, bristly coat, just like a brush. We can scrub the floor with you."

"Right ho!" said Pup. And Puss took the soap and the pail of water, and knelt down on the floor. Then she scrubbed the whole floor with Pup.

By now the floor was all wet, and it wasn't any too clean either.

"We ought to rub it over with something dry," said Puss.

"I'll tell you what," said Pup. "I'm sopping wet, but you're dry, and your fur is nice and soft. It'll make a lovely floorcloth. I'll dry the floor with you."

So he took hold of Puss and dried the whole floor with her.

The floor was now washed and dried, but Puss and Pup were all wet and terribly dirty from having been used to wash the floor.

"Well, we do look a sight!" they both said, looking at each other. "We've got the floor clean all right, but now look at us! We can't possibly stay like this. Everybody will laugh. We'll have to be sent to the wash."

"Let's wash each other, like they do at the laundry," said Pup. "You wash me, and when I'm done, I'll wash you."

"Very well," said Puss.

They filled the tub of water and took a scrubbing-board. Pup got into the tub and Puss washed him. She rubbed him so much on the scrubbing-board that Pup begged her not to press so hard, as his legs were getting all tangled up.

When Pup finished, Puss got into the tub and Pup scrubbed and squeezed her so much that she begged him not to press her so hard on the scrubbing-board in case he made a hole in her fur.

Then they wrung each other out.

"Now we'll hang ourselves out to dry," said Puss. So they put out the clothes-line.

"First I'll hang you up on the line, and when you're up, you can get down and hang me up," Pup told Puss.

So Pup took hold of Puss and hung her up, just like washing. They didn't need any pegs, because they could hold on to the line with their claws. Once Puss was on the line, she jumped down and hung up Pup.

By now the two of them were hanging nicely and the sun was shining brightly.

"The sun's shining on us," cried Pup. "We'll soon be dry." No sooner had he said this than it began to rain.

"Oh, dear, it's raining!" shouted Puss and Pup. "The washing will get wet. Let's take it down!"

They jumped down quickly and ran to the cottage for shelter.

"Is it still raining?" asked Puss.

"It's stopped," said Pup, and sure enough the sun was out again.

"Let's hang the washing out again, then," said Puss.

So they hung themselves on the line a second time. First Pup put Puss up, and as soon as she was hanging up she jumped down and put up Pup. So they both hung on the line, just like washing, and were very pleased at the way the sun shone and made such a good drying day. But then it began to rain again.

"It's raining! Our washing will get wet!" cried Puss and Pup. And they ran for shelter. Soon the sun came out again, and again they hung each other up on the clothes-line. Then it started raining, and off they scampered. Then the sun came out again and they hung themselves up again, and so it went on till the evening. By that time they were both quite dry.

"Our washing's dry," they said. "Let's put it in the basket."

So they clambered into the basket. But then they felt so sleepy that they both fell asleep. And they slept in the basket right through until the next morning.

Can Men Be Such Fools as All That?

---◆---

I was nurse to the little Duke of Chinon, who lived in the great grim castle on the hill above the town where the Rag-picker's Son lived. The little Duke, of course, had everything that the poor boy hadn't: fine clothes to wear, white bread and chicken to eat, and a pedigree spaniel called Hubert for a play-fellow.

Except for all these differences, the two boys were as like as two peas; when I took the little Duke walking by the river, and we happened to meet the Rag-picker's Son, you could not have told one from the other, if one hadn't worn satin and the other rags, while one had a dirty face and hands and the other was as clean as a new pin. Everybody remarked on it.

The little Duke used to look longingly at the poor boy, though, for he was allowed to splash about in the water of the river as he pleased; and the water of the Loire is more beautiful to splash about in than any water in France, for it is as clear as honey, and has the brightest gold sand-bed you can imagine; and when you get out of the town, it runs between sandy shores, where green willows grow, and flowers of all sorts. But it was against my orders to let the little Duke play in the water, and I had to obey them, though I was sorry for him; for I knew what boys like.

One day as we were out walking, the Duke's spaniel, Hubert, ran up to the Rag-picker's Son's mongrel, Jacques, and they touched noses and made friends. And the Duke and the poor

boy smiled at each other and said, "Hullo!" After that, when
we met, the boys always nodded, or winked, or made some sign
of friendship; and one day the Rag-picker's Son jerked his
thumb at the river, as much as to say, "Come in and play with
me!"

The Duke looked at me, and I shook my head, so the Duke
shook his. But he was cross with me for the rest of the day.

The next day I missed him, and there was a great hullabaloo
all over the castle. I and his guardian and all his attendants
went down to the town to find him; and asked everybody we
met if they had seen him; and presently we met the Rag-picker,
who said, "Yes, I saw him an hour ago, going along the river-
bank with my son." And we all ran along the bank, the Rag-
picker too, and most of the townsfolk behind us.

A mile along the bank, there they were, the two boys, standing in the middle of the river as bare as when they were born,
splashing about and screaming with laughter, and on the shore
lay a little heap of clothes, rags and fine linen all thrown down
anyhow together. We were all very angry with the boys, and
called and shouted to them to come out of the water; and they
shouted back that they wouldn't. At last the Rag-picker waded
in and fetched them out by the scruffs of their necks. And there
they stood before us, naked and grinning and full of fun, and
just as the Duke's guardian was going to scold his charge, and
the Rag-picker to scold his son, they suddenly found themselves
in a pickle! For without their clothes, washed clean by the
river, they were so exactly alike, that we didn't know which
was which. And the boys saw that we didn't and grinned more
than ever.

"Now then, my boy!" said the Rag-picker to one of them.
But the boy he spoke to did not answer, for he knew if he talked
it would give the game away.

And the Duke's guardian said to the other boy, "Come, mon-
seigneur!" But that boy too shook his head and kept mum.

Then I had a bright idea, and said to the boys, "Put on your

clothes!'' for I thought that would settle it. But the two boys picked up the clothes as they came: one of them put on the ragged shirt and the satin coat, and the other put on the fine shirt and the ragged coat. So we were no better off than before.

Then the Rag-picker and the Duke's guardian lost their tempers, and raised their sticks and gave each of the boys three strokes, thinking that might help; but all it did was to make them squeal, and when a boy squeals it doesn't matter if he's a Duke or a beggar, the sound is just the same.

"This is dreadful," said the Duke's guardian; "for all we know, we shall get the boys mixed for ever, and I shall take the Rag-picker's Son back to the castle, and the Duke will grow up as the Rag-picker's Son. Is there no way of telling which is which? Can we all be such fools as that?"

Just as we were scratching our heads and cudgelling our brains, and wondering what on earth to do next, there came a sound of yelps and barks; and out of the willows ran Jacques and Hubert, who had been off on their own, playing together. They came racing towards us joyously, and straight as a die Jacques jumped up and licked the face of the boy in the satin coat, while Hubert licked the boy in the ragged jacket.

So then there was no doubt about it. We made the boys change their coats, and the Rag-picker marched his son home to bed, and the guardian did the same with the Duke. And that night the Duke and the poor boy had exactly the same supper to go to sleep on; in other words, nothing and plenty of it.

But how had the dogs known in the twink of an eye what we hadn't known at all? Can men be such fools as all that?

The Little Hare and the Tiger

◆

Everyone in the forest was afraid of the extremely fierce tiger who, every day without fail, would come on his regular prowl and carry off not just one animal or two, but three or four or even more. For he was a very greedy tiger. No one could ever feel safe, for no one knew who was to be the next victim.

One day the jackal had a bright idea. He called a meeting of the animals and spoke to them in the following terms.

"Fellow animals," he began. "I would like to suggest that we undertake to send the tiger one animal regularly every day for his dinner. You know how fat and lazy he is getting. So if he gets his regular daily feast guaranteed by us, he won't have to come stalking through the forest killing everyone he meets." Now the jackal was very cunning. He was thinking to himself, "We'll send all the *smaller* animals to the tiger first and then I'll be safe for a long time to come."

The tiger himself thought this was an excellent plan and all the other animals agreed too—all, that is, except the little hare. When he heard that he was to be first to be the tiger's dinner, he wasn't at all pleased. Not surprising, of course. So the little hare spoke up and said, "No, I'm not going. No, no, no, a thousand times no."

This got the animals very worried indeed. They were afraid that if they kept the tiger waiting, he would come stalking along in his usual manner and carry off several of them. But try as they might they simply could not persuade the little hare. He just sat, with a thoughtful look on his face, muttering, "No, no, no." In the distance they could hear the tiger roaring impatiently. Luckily he thought his dinner was on the way and he felt too lazy to come and fetch it himself. Suddenly, the little hare, who had been growing more and more thoughtful, sprang and shouted, "I'm off," and off he ran, as fast as lightning, maybe even a little faster.

The other animals gave a sigh of relief because they thought the little hare had at last been persuaded to go to the tiger, and present himself as the first dinner. Nothing of the kind, of course. But mind you, he did go to the tiger's cave, right inside, too, but just outside the reach of the tiger's paws.

The tiger, very lazy, had been having a little grumbling sort of snooze. When he saw the little hare, he growled, "Come here, you pathetic little creature. You're late enough already."

The little hare burst into tears. "I'm so sorry, Tiger, to be so thin and be such a poor dinner for you. My brother was so beautifully fat."

"Your brother!" roared the tiger. "Your fat brother, you say? Then why didn't *he* come, instead of you?" And this made him angrier and hungrier than ever.

"Well, he did, actually," sobbed the little hare. "That is, he did start out to get here, but they unfortunately got him on the way. Boo, hoo!" and he gave a loud wail.

"Who got him?" roared the tiger, so loudly that the ceiling of the cave nearly burst.

"The other tiger," sobbed the little hare. "You know, the one who lives in that hole in the bushes."

"Lead me to him," thundered the tiger. "I'll teach him to eat up all the fat hares and leave the skinny little ones like you."

"Very well," said the little hare, "come this way, Tiger, and I will lead you to his den."

The tiger, like all other cats, could not see too well in the bright sunlight and he peered about suspiciously as he followed

the little hare through the tall jungle grass. All of a sudden, without any warning whatsoever, the little hare darted off into some bushes. "This way, Tiger," he called out. And the great beast followed him and found himself in an open space by the side of a deep hole, or what looked like a deep hole. "This is the other tiger's den," said the little hare in a very scared voice. "The one that ate my fat brother."

The tiger went up to the very edge of the hole and leaned

over. Looking up at him was the face of the most ferocious tiger he had ever seen.

"Grrrrrr . . ." roared the tiger. "I'm going to teach you a lesson you will never forget," and he jumped and —splash! Down and down he went, for the hole was a deep, deep well filled with shining water, clear as a looking-glass, and the tiger looking up at him had really been his own greedy self. And so that was the end of *him*. For he never, ever got out of that well again.

And as for the little hare, he went back and told all the other animals that they had nothing more to fear from the greedy tiger. And he was acclaimed the most heroic little hare in the whole forest.

Six Foolish Fishermen

Alf, Bill, Clem, Dick, Ed and Fred were six brothers who were all very keen fishermen.

One fine morning they decided to go down to the river to see who could catch the most fish.

Alf said he would fish from his boat, Bill from a raft, Clem from a bridge over the river, Dick from a tree overhanging the river, and Ed from a little island in the middle of the river. Fred said:

"I shall walk along the bank of the river and fish."

They fished all through that sunny morning, they all caught lots of fish and they were all very pleased with themselves.

But Alf was worried about one thing, one rather important thing. As all the brothers had been fishing in different places he wondered whether they were all safe and sound. "Perhaps Clem has fallen off the bridge and got drowned," he thought. "Or maybe Dick has slipped off that tree-trunk. I had better count all us brothers to see if we are all here" and he started to count: "There's Bill on the raft, that makes one. There's Clem on the bridge, that's two. I can see Dick on the tree, that's three, there's Ed on the island, that's four. And Fred on the bank, that's five. But we are six. Good gracious me! One brother has been lost." He was so upset, he forgot to count himself.

Bill, on the raft, heard him. "Have we really lost one?" he asked and he too began to count.

"There's Clem on the bridge. That makes one. Dick is on

the tree. That's two. I spy Ed on the island. That's three. And there's Fred on the bank, that's four. Oh yes, of course, that's Alf looking worried in the boat, that's five. Five! Where's the sixth? Oh dear, we've lost one."

Clem spotted him from the bridge. "I'm going to have a re-count," he said. "There's Dick on that branch, that's one. Ed is quite visible on the island, that's two. Fred is on the bank, that's three. Alf is still there in his boat, that's four, and Bill is floating towards me on his raft, making five. Oh goodness me! Only five! We have indeed lost one."

He was so upset that Dick counted them again just to make sure, but he too only found five. And Ed and Fred weren't any luckier either when they checked.

So they all left the spots from where they had been fishing and ran up and down the river-bank trying to find the body of their unfortunate drowned brother.

Just then a boy came strolling along the bank with his fishing-line and an empty basket. He too had been fishing but had not caught a single thing.

"Why do you all look so worried?" he asked the brothers. "You all seem to have had a very good morning's fishing."

"Because one of our brothers has been drowned," they explained in great distress. "There were six of us when we started out, and now there are only five."

The boy made a quick count and saw there *were* six brothers.

"Look," he said, "I can help you find your lost brother. When I tickle each of you on the neck, I want you to count." He went up to Alf and tickled him. "One!" cried Alf, laughing. Then he went up to Bill and tickled *his* neck. "Two!" cried Bill. And "Three!" shouted Clem. And "Four!" laughed Dick. And "Five!" chuckled Ed. And "Six!" shrieked Fred.

And "Six!" all the brothers roared in unison, realising they were all safe and sound. They all embraced one another and shouted for joy. And in gratitude to the boy they gave him all the fish they had caught.

The Ugsome Thing

◆

There was once a monster called the Ugsome Thing. He was round and fat and scaly and he had long teeth twisted like sticks of barley sugar. He lived in a castle and had many servants to wait on him. They had to clean his castle and cook his food and till his fields and tend his flocks and herds. Though they worked hard, he never paid them a penny in wages.

The Ugsome Thing had a magic power, and if he could make anyone lose his temper, that person became his slave and had to obey him.

At this time, the Ugsome Thing had all the servants he wanted except for one—he had not a good washerwoman. His clothes were often dirty and badly ironed. Now, as he went through the village near his castle, he passed a cottage garden which was full, on a Monday, of the whitest clothes he had ever seen. They were like snow, blowing and billowing on the line stretched between two apple trees. He decided to make the old woman who lived there come and do his washing. It would be very simple. He only had to make her lose her temper and she would be in his power.

So one Monday morning, when her clothes-line was full of the whitest wash possible, he cut the line with his knife and the snowy clothes lay tumbled on the dirty grass. Surely that would make her lose her temper.

When the old woman saw what had happened, she came

running out of the door, and instead of losing her temper she said quietly:

"Well! Well! Well! The chimney has been smoking this morning and I'm sure some smuts must have blown on my washing. Anyway, it will be a good idea to wash it again. How lucky that the line broke just this morning and no other!"

So she picked up armfuls of the dirty clothes and went back to the wash-house, singing as she went.

The Ugsome Thing was very angry and he gnashed his barley sugar teeth, but he soon thought of another idea to make her lose her temper.

On Tuesday the Ugsome Thing visited the old woman again. He saw that she had milked her cow, Daisy, and that the milk stood in a pan in the dairy. He turned the whole pan of milk sour. Surely that would make her lose her temper.

When the old woman saw the pan of sour milk she said:

"Well! Well! Well! Now I shall have to make it into cream cheese and that will be a treat for my grandchildren when they come to tea. They love having cream cheese on their scones. How lucky the milk turned sour just today and no other!"

The Ugsome Thing was very angry and he gnashed his barley sugar teeth, but he soon thought of another idea to make her lose her temper.

On Wednesday the Ugsome Thing visited the old woman again. He turned all the hollyhocks in her garden into thistles, the red ones and the pink ones and the double yellow ones. She was very proud of her garden. Surely that would make her lose her temper.

"Well! Well! Well!" said the old woman when she saw thistles growing by the wall instead of hollyhocks. "I was going to pick a bunch of hollyhocks today for my friend's birthday, but now I shall make her a pin-cushion instead, and stuff it with thistledown."

So she made a velvet pin-cushion and stuffed it with thistle-down and embroidered a flower on it. It looked nearly as pretty as the hollyhocks and lasted much longer.

"How lucky I am that I noticed all those thistles just today and no other," she said, as she sewed up the pin-cushion.

The Ugsome Thing was very angry and gnashed his barley sugar teeth, but he soon thought of another idea to make her lose her temper.

On Thursday the Ugsome Thing stretched a piece of string across the stairs, hoping that the old woman would trip over it and fall. Surely that would make her lose her temper.

The old woman did fall, and hurt her knee, and had to hop on one leg to the shed to milk Daisy the cow.

"Well! Well! Well!" said the old woman. "I can't do any housework today. I shall lie on the sofa and get on with my patchwork quilt. What a nice change that will be! I may even get it finished. How lucky I am that I tripped over just today, and no other!"

The Ugsome Thing was very angry and gnashed his barley sugar teeth, but he soon thought of another idea to make her lose her temper.

On Friday the Ugsome Thing visited the old woman again. He saw her going to the hen-house to collect the eggs. She had three white hens and they had each laid an egg. As she was walking past the apple tree, he flipped a branch in her face and she dropped the bowl and broke the eggs. Surely that would make her lose her temper.

"Well! Well! Well!" said the old woman. "Now I shall have to have scrambled eggs for dinner and supper, and scrambled eggs are my favourite food. How lucky I am that the eggs broke just today and no other!"

Now the Ugsome Thing was very angry indeed and he gnashed his barley sugar teeth, but he soon thought of another idea to make her lose her temper. This idea was a very nasty one, because he was very, very angry indeed.

On Saturday the Ugsome Thing set the old woman's cottage on fire. Surely that would make her lose her temper. The flames

shot up the walls and soon the thatched roof caught fire.

"Well! Well! Well!" said the old woman. "That's the last of my old cottage. I was fond of it, but it was falling to pieces and the roof let in the rain and there were holes in the floor."

When the Ugsome Thing came along to see if the old woman had lost her temper, he found her busy baking potatoes in the hot ashes, and handing them round to the village children.

"Have a potato?" she said to the Ugsome Thing, holding one out on the point of a stick.

It smelled so good that the Ugsome Thing took it and crammed it into his mouth whole, because he was very greedy, and some of it went down the wrong way. He choked so hard with rage and hot potato that he burst like a balloon and there was nothing left but a piece of shrivelled, scaly, greenish skin. A little boy threw it on the fire, thinking it was an old rag, and it burned with a spluttering yellow flame.

By this time, most of the people in the village were lining up to have a baked potato, and while they waited they planned how they could help the old woman.

"I'll build the walls of a new cottage," said one.

"I'll make the roof," said another.

"I'll put in the windows," said a third.

"I'll paper the walls," said a fourth.

"We'll give her a carpet—sheets—a blanket—a kettle—" said the women. By the time all the potatoes were cooked and eaten, her friends had promised the old woman all she needed for a new cottage.

The new cottage was not old and tumbledown like the first one, but dry and comfortable with a sunny porch. Daisy had a new shed and the dog a new kennel. Only the cat was disappointed as there were no mice for her to chase. There were no holes for the mice to live in.

The Woman Who Always Argued

Once upon a time, there was an old man and an old woman. The man was all right. It was the woman who was the trouble.

Whatever anyone said, she said the opposite. If the fishmonger said, "I've some good herrings today," she said, "No, I want sprats." If the butcher said, "I've got lamb chops today," she said, "No, I want beef." If anyone opened a window, she shut it. If someone shut it, she opened it. She vowed that hens were ducks, and cats were dogs, and when it was raining she said it was snowing.

As for her poor old husband, what trouble he had. He was with her all the time, you see, because they did the farming together. So you can imagine he was very tired of it.

One morning they went across the bridge to look at their cornfield.

"Ah," said the man. "The corn will be ready by Tuesday."

"Monday," said the woman.

"Very well then, Monday," said the man. "I'll get John and Eric to help harvest it."

"No you won't," said the woman. "You'll get James and Robert."

"All right," said the man. "James and Robert. We'll start at seven."

"At six," said his wife.

"At six," agreed the man. "The weather will be good for it."

"It will be bad," she said. "It will pour."

"Well, whether it rains or shines," said the man, getting fed up, "whether we do it Monday at seven or Tuesday at six, we'll cut it with scythes."

"Shears," said his wife.

"Shears?" said the man, amazed. "Cut the corn with shears? What are you talking about! We'll cut with scythes!" (For with shears, you see, you have to bend down and go snip, snip, at one tiny bit after another. But with the lovely curved scythe, you go *swoosh!* and half the corn falls down flat.) "We'll cut with scythes!" said the man.

"Shears!" said the woman.

They went over the bridge, still arguing.

"Scythes!" said the man.

"Shears!" said the woman.

So angry was the woman that the man was arguing back, that she didn't look where she was going, and she fell off the bridge into the water. When she bobbed up again, you'd think she'd shout "Help!" but not her. She shouted "Shears!" and the man only just had time to shout "Scythes!" before she bobbed back again.

Up she came again, and "Shears!" she shouted. The man yelled back "Scythes!" and she disappeared again. She came up again once more, and this time there was so much water in her mouth, because she would keep opening it to argue, that she couldn't say anything at all, so as her head went back again she stuck out her hand and with the fingers she silently went snip-snip, like shears above the water, snip-snip. Then she was gone.

"Stupid old woman!" said the man, stamping his foot. "Stupid, obstinate, argumentative old woman!"

He went to the village to get his friends to help him find her. They all came back to the bridge, and searched in the water. But she wasn't there.

"If the water has carried her away," said one of them, "she

will be downstream. That is the way the river flows, and everything in the water must go with the river."

So they went downstream and looked, but they couldn't find her.

Suddenly the old man shouted, "What a fool I am! Everything else in the water would go with the river, it's true. But

not my wife! She's bound to do the opposite. She'll be floating the other way, mark my words!"

So they ran up the stream, and sure enough, there she was, the opposite way to everything else. And what do you know, she was insisting on floating right *up* the waterfall!

The Magician's Heart

◆

We all have our weaknesses. Mine is mulberries. Yours, perhaps, motor-cars. Professor Taykin's was christenings—royal christenings. He always expected to be asked to the christening parties of all the little royal babies, and of course he never was, because he was not a lord, or a duke, or a seller of bacon and tea, or anything really high class, but merely a wicked magician, who by economy and strict attention to customers had worked up a very good business of his own. He had not always been wicked. He was born quite good, I believe, and his old nurse, who had long since married a farmer and retired into the calm of country life, always used to say that he was the duckiest little boy in a plaid frock with the dearest little fat legs. But he had changed since he was a boy, as a good many other people do—perhaps it was his trade. I dare say you've noticed that cobblers are usually thin, and brewers are generally fat, and magicians are almost always wicked.

Well, his weakness (for christenings) grew stronger and stronger because it was never indulged, and at last he 'took the bull into his own hands' as the Irish footman at the palace said, and went to a christening without being asked. It was a very grand party given by the King of the Fortunate Islands, and the little Prince was christened Fortunatus. No one took any notice of Professor Taykin. They were too polite to turn him out, but they made him wish he'd never come. He felt quite an outsider, as indeed he was, and this made him furious. So that

182

when all the bright, light, laughing fairy godmothers were crowding round the blue satin cradle, and giving gifts of beauty and strength and goodness to the baby, the Magician suddenly did a very difficult charm (in his head, like you do mental arithmetic), and said:

"Young Forty may be all that, but I say he shall be the stupidest prince in the world," and on that he vanished in a puff of red smoke with a smell like the Fifth of November in a back garden on Streatham Hill, and as he left no address the King of the Fortunate Islands couldn't prosecute him for high treason.

Taykin was very glad to think that he had made such a lot of people unhappy—the whole court was in tears when he left, including the baby—and he looked in the papers for another royal christening, so that he could go to that and make a lot more people miserable. And there was one fixed for the very next Wednesday. The Magician went to that too, disguised as a wealthy merchant.

This time the baby was a girl. Taykin kept close to the pink velvet cradle, and when all the nice qualities in the world had been given to the Princess he suddenly said: "Little Aura may be all that, but I say she shall be the ugliest princess in all the world."

And instantly she was. It was terrible. And she had been such a beautiful baby too. Everyone had been saying that she was the most beautiful baby they had ever seen. This sort of thing is often said at christenings.

Having uglified the unfortunate little Princess the Magician did the spell (in his mind, just as you do your spelling) to make himself vanish, but to his horror there was no red smoke and no smell of fireworks, and there he was, still, where he now very much wished not to be. Because one of the fairies there had seen, just one second too late to save the Princess, what he was up to, and had made a strong little charm in a great hurry to prevent his vanishing. This fairy was a white Witch, and of

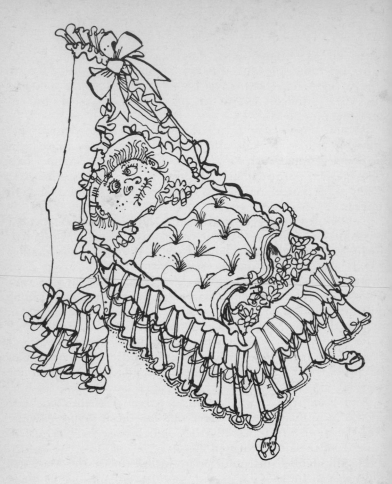

course you know that White Magic is much stronger than Black Magic, as well as more suited for drawing-room performances. So there the Magician stood, "looking like a thunder-struck pig", as someone unkindly said, and the dear White Witch bent down and kissed the baby Princess.

"There!" she said, "you can keep that kiss till you want it.

When the time comes you'll know what to do with it. The Magician can't vanish, sire. You'd better arrest him."

"Arrest that person," said the King, pointing to Taykin. "I suppose your charms are of a permanent nature, madam."

"Quite," said the Fairy, "at least they never go till there's no longer any use for them."

So the Magician was shut up in an enormously high tower, and allowed to play with magic; but none of his spells could act outside the tower so he was never able to pass the extra double guard that watched outside night and day. The King would have liked to have the Magician executed but the White Witch warned him that this would never do.

"Don't you see," she said, "he's the only person who can make the Princess beautiful again. And he'll do it some day. But don't you go asking him to do it. He'll never do anything to oblige you. He's that sort of man."

So the years rolled on. The Magician stayed in the tower and did magic and was very bored, for it is dull to take white rabbits out of your hat, and your hat out of nothing when there's no one to see you.

Prince Fortunatus was such a stupid little boy that he got lost quite early in the story, and went about the country saying his name was James, which it wasn't. A baker's wife found him and adopted him, and sold the diamond buttons of his little overcoat for three hundred pounds, and as she was a very honest woman she put two hundred away for James to have when he grew up.

The years rolled on. Aura continued to be hideous, and she was very unhappy, till on her twentieth birthday her married cousin Belinda came to see her. Now Belinda had been made ugly in her cradle too, so she could sympathize as no one else could.

"But I got out of it all right, and so will you," said Belinda. "I'm sure the first thing to do is to find a magician."

"Father banished them all twenty years ago," said Aura

behind her veil, "all but the one who uglified me."

"Then I should go to him," said beautiful Belinda. "Dress up as a beggar maid, and give him fifty pounds to do it. Not more, or he may suspect that you're not a beggar maid. It will be great fun. I'd go with you only I promised Bellamant faithfully that I'd be home to lunch." And off she went in her mother-of-pearl coach, leaving Aura to look through the bound volumes of The Perfect Lady in the palace library, to find out the proper costume for a beggar maid.

Now that very morning the Magician's old nurse had packed up a ham and some eggs and some honey and some apples and a sweet bunch of old-fashioned flowers, and borrowed the baker's boy to hold the horse for her, and started off to see the Magician. It was forty years since she'd seen him, but she loved him still, and now she thought she could do him a good turn. She asked in the town for his address, and learned that he lived in the Black Tower.

"But you'd best be careful," the townsfolk said; "he's a spiteful chap."

"Bless you," said the old nurse, "he won't hurt me as I nursed him when he was a babe, in a plaid frock with the dearest little fat legs you ever did see."

So she got to the tower, and the guards let her through. Taykin was almost pleased to see her—remember he had had no visitors for twenty years—and he was quite pleased to see the ham and the honey.

"But where did I put them heggs?" said the nurse, "and the apples—I must have left them at home after all."

She had. But the Magician just waved his hand in the air, and there was a basket of apples that hadn't been there before. The eggs he took out of her bonnet, the folds of her shawl, and even from his own mouth, just like a conjuror does. Only of course he was a real Magician.

"Lor!" said she, "it's like magic."

"It is magic," said he. "That's my trade. It's quite a pleasure

186

to have an audience again. I've lived here alone for twenty years. It's very lonely, especially of an evening."

"Can't you get out?" said the nurse.

"No. King's orders must be respected, but it's a dog's life." He sniffed, made himself a magic handkerchief out of empty air, and wiped his eyes.

"Take an apprentice, my dear," said the nurse.

"And teach him my magic? Not me."

"Suppose you got one so stupid he couldn't learn?"

"That would be all right—but it's no use advertising for a stupid person—you'd get no answers."

"You needn't advertise," said the nurse; and she went out and brought in James, who was really the Prince of the Fortunate Islands, and also the baker's boy she had brought with her to hold the horse's head.

"Now, James," she said, "you'd like to be apprenticed, wouldn't you?"

"Yes," said the poor stupid boy.

"Then give the gentleman your money, James."

James did.

"My last doubts vanish," said the Magician, "he is stupid. Nurse, let us celebrate the occasion with a little drop of something. Not before the boy because of setting an example. James, wash up. Not here, silly: in the back kitchen."

So James washed up, and as he was very clumsy he happened to break a little bottle of essence of dreams that was on the shelf, and instantly there floated up from the washing-up water the vision of a princess more beautiful than the day—so beautiful that even James could not help seeing how beautiful she was, and holding out his arms to her as she came floating through the air above the kitchen sink. But when he held out his arms she vanished. He sighed and washed up harder than ever.

"I wish I wasn't so stupid," he said and then there was a knock at the door. James wiped his hands and opened. Someone stood there in very picturesque rags and tatters. "Please," said someone, who was of course the Princess, "is Professor Taykin at home?"

"Walk in, please," said James.

"My snakes alive!" said Taykin, "what a day we're having. Three visitors in one morning. How kind of you to call. Won't you take a chair?"

"I hoped," said the veiled Princess, "that you'd give me something else to take."

"A glass of wine," said Taykin. "You'll take a glass of wine?"

"No, thank you," said the beggar maid who was the Princess.

"Then take . . . take your veil off," said the nurse, "or you won't feel the benefit of it when you go out."

"I can't," said Aura, "it wouldn't be safe."

"Too beautiful, eh?" said the Magician. "Still—you're quite safe here."

"Can you do magic?" she abruptly asked.

"A little," said he ironically.

"Well," said she, "it's like this. I'm so ugly no one can bear to look at me. And I want to go as kitchen-maid to the palace. They want a cook and a scullion and a kitchen-maid. I thought perhaps you'd give me something to make me pretty. I'm only a poor beggar maid . . . it would be a great thing to me if . . ."

"Go along with you," said Taykin, very cross indeed. "I never give to beggars."

"Here's twopence," whispered poor James, pressing it into her hand, "it's all I've got left."

"Thank you," she whispered back. "You are good."

And to the Magician she said:

"I happen to have fifty pounds. I'll give it you for a new face."

"Done," cried Taykin. "Here's another stupid one!" He grabbed the money, waved his wand, and then and there before the astonished eyes of the nurse and the apprentice the ugly beggar maid became the loveliest princess in the world.

"Lor!" said the nurse.

"My dream!" cried the apprentice.

"Please," said the Princess, "can I have a looking-glass?"
The apprentice ran to unhook the one that hung over the
kitchen sink, and handed it to her. "Oh," she said, "how very
pretty I am. How can I thank you?"

"Quite easily," said the Magician, "beggar maid as you are,
I hereby offer you my hand and heart."

He put his hand into his waistcoat and pulled out his heart.
It was fat and pink, and the Princess did not like the look of it.

"Thank you very much," said she, "but I'd rather not."

"But I insist," said Taykin.

"But really, your offer . . ."

"Most handsome, I'm sure," said the nurse.

"My affections are engaged," said the Princess, looking down.
"I can't marry you."

"Am I to take this as a refusal?" asked Taykin; and the
Princess said she feared that he was.

"Very well, then," he said, "I shall see you home, and ask
your father about it. He'll not let you refuse an offer like this.
Nurse, come and tie my necktie."

So he went out, and the nurse with him.

Then the Princess told the apprentice in a very great hurry
who she was.

"It would never do," she said, "for him to see me home. He'd
find out that I was the Princess, and he'd uglify me again in no
time."

"He shan't see you home," said James. "I may be stupid but
I'm strong too."

"How brave you are," said Aura admiringly, "but I'd rather
slip away quietly, without any fuss. Can't you undo the patent
lock of that door?" The apprentice tried but he was too stupid,
and the Princess was not strong enough.

"I'm sorry," said the apprentice who was a prince. "I can't
undo the door, but when he does I'll hold him and you can get
away. I dreamed of you this morning," he added.

"I dreamed of you too," said she, "but you were different."

"Perhaps," said poor James sadly, "the person you dreamed about wasn't stupid, and I am."

"Are you really?" cried the Princess. "I am so glad!"

"That's rather unkind, isn't it?" said he.

"No; because if that's all that makes you different from the man I dreamed about I can soon make that all right."

And with that she put her hands on his shoulders and kissed him. And at her kiss his stupidness passed away like a cloud, and he became as clever as anyone need be; and besides knowing all the ordinary lessons he would have learned if he had stayed at home in his palace, he knew all the geography of his father's kingdom, and the exports and imports and the conditions of politics. And he knew also that the Princess loved him.

So he caught her in his arms and kissed her, and they were very happy, and told each other over and over again what a beautiful world it was, and how wonderful it was that they should have found each other, seeing that the world is not only beautiful but rather large.

"That first one was a magic kiss, you know," said she. "My fairy godmother gave it to me, and I've been keeping it all these years for you. You must get away from here and come to the palace. Oh, you'll manage it—you're clever now."

"Yes," he said, "I am clever now. I can undo the lock for you. Go, my dear, go before he comes back."

So the Princess went. And only just in time; for as she went out of one door Taykin came in at the other.

He was furious to find her gone; and I should not like to write down the things he said to his apprentice when he found that James had been so stupid as to open the door for her. They were not polite things at all.

He tried to follow her. But the Princess had warned the guards, and he could not get out.

"Oh," he cried, "if only my old magic would work outside this tower. I'd soon be even with her."

And then in a strange, confused, yet quite sure way, he felt that the spell that held him, the White Witch's spell, was dissolved.

"To the palace!" he cried; and rushing to the cauldron that hung over the fire he leaped into it, leaped out in the form of a red lion, and disappeared.

Without a moment's hesitation the Prince, who was his apprentice, followed him, calling out the same words and leaping into the same cauldron, while the poor nurse screamed and wrung her hands. As he touched the liquor in the cauldron he felt that he was not quite himself. He was, in fact, a green dragon. He felt himself vanish—a most uncomfortable sensation—and reappeared, with a suddenness that took his breath away, in his own form and at the back door of the palace.

The time had been short, but already the Magician had succeeded in obtaining an engagement as palace cook. How he did it without references I don't know. Perhaps he made the references by magic as he had made the eggs and the apples and the handkerchief.

Taykin's astonishment and annoyance at being followed by his faithful apprentice were soon soothed, for he saw that a stupid scullion would be of great use. Of course he had no idea that James had been made clever by a kiss.

"But how are you going to cook?" asked the apprentice. "You don't know how!"

"I shall cook," said Taykin, "as I do everything else—by magic." And he did. I wish I had time to tell you how he turned out a hot dinner of seventeen courses from totally empty saucepans, how James looked in a cupboard for spices and found it empty, and how next moment the nurse walked out of it. The Magician had been so long alone that he seemed to revel in the luxury of showing off to someone, and he leaped about from one cupboard to another, produced cats and cockatoos out of empty jars, and made mice and rabbits disappear and reappear till James's head was in a whirl, for all his cleverness; and the nurse, as she washed up, wept tears of pure joy at her boy's wonderful skill.

"All this excitement's bad for my heart, though," Taykin said at last, and pulling his heart out of his chest, he put it on a shelf, and as he did so his magic note-book fell from his breast and the apprentice picked it up. Taykin did not see him do it; he was busy making the kitchen lamp fly about the room like a pigeon.

It was just then that the Princess came in, looking more lovely than ever in a simple little morning frock of white chiffon and diamonds.

"The beggar maid," said Taykin, "looking like a princess! I'll marry her just the same."

"I've come to give the orders for dinner," she said; and then she saw who it was, and gave one little cry and stood still, trembling.

"To order the dinner," said the nurse. "Then you're—"

"Yes," said Aura, "I'm the Princess."

"You're the Princess," said the Magician. "Then I'll marry you all the more. And if you say no I'll uglify you as the word leaves your lips. Oh yes—you think I've just been amusing myself over my cooking—but I've really been brewing the strongest spell in the world. Marry me—or drink—"

The Princess shuddered at these dreadful words.

"Drink, or marry me," said the Magician. "If you marry me you shall be beautiful for ever."

"Ah," said the nurse, "he's a match even for a Princess."

"I'll tell papa," said the Princess, sobbing.

"No you won't," said Taykin. "Your father will never know. If you won't marry me you shall drink this and become my scullery maid—my hideous scullery maid—and wash up for ever in the lonely tower."

He caught her by the wrist.

"Stop!" cried the apprentice who was a prince.

"Stop? Me? Nonsense! Pooh!" said the Magician.

"Stop, I say!" said James, who was Fortunatus. "I've got your heart!" He had—and he held it up in one hand, and in the other a cooking knife.

"One step nearer that lady," said he, "and in goes the knife."

The Magician positively skipped in his agony and terror.

"I say, look out!" he cried. "Be careful what you're doing. Accidents happen so easily! Suppose your foot slipped! Then no apologies would meet the case. That's my heart you've got there. My life's bound up in it."

"I know. That's often the case with people's hearts," said Fortunatus. "We've got you, my dear sir, on toast. My Princess, might I trouble you to call the guards."

The Magician did not dare to resist, so the guards arrested him. The nurse, though in floods of tears, managed to serve up a very good plain dinner, and after dinner the Magician was brought before the King.

Now the King, as soon as he had seen that his daughter had been made so beautiful, had caused a large number of princes to be fetched by telephone. He was anxious to get her married at once in case she turned ugly again. So before he could do justice to the Magician he had to settle which of the princes was to marry the Princess. He had chosen the Prince of the Diamond Mountains, a very nice steady young man with a good income. But when he suggested the match to the Princess she declined it, and the Magician, who was standing at the foot of the throne steps loaded with chains, clattered forward and said:

"Your Majesty, will you spare my life if I tell you something you don't know?"

The King, who was a very inquisitive man, said "Yes."

"Then know," said Taykin, "that the Princess won't marry your choice because she's made one of her own—my apprentice."

The Princess meant to have told her father this when she had got him alone and in a good temper. But now he was in a bad temper, and in full audience.

The apprentice was dragged in, and all the Princess's agonized pleadings only got this out of the King:

"All right. I won't hang him. He shall be best man at your wedding."

Then the King took his daughter's hand and set her in the middle of the hall, and set the Prince of the Diamond Mountains on her right and the apprentice on her left. Then he said:

"I will spare the life of this aspiring youth on your left if you'll promise never to speak to him again, and if you'll promise to marry the gentleman on your right before tea this afternoon."

The wretched Princess looked at her lover, and his lips formed the word 'Promise'.

So she said "I promise never to speak to the gentleman on my left and to marry the gentleman on my right before tea today," and held out her hand to the Prince of the Diamond Mountains.

Then suddenly, in the twinkling of an eye, the Prince of the Diamond Mountains was on her left, and her hand was held by her own Prince, who stood at her right hand. And yet nobody seemed to have moved. It was the purest and most high-class magic.

"Dished," cried the King, "absolutely dished!"

"A mere trifle," said the apprentice modestly. "I've got Taykin's magic recipe book, as well as his heart."

"Well, we must make the best of it, I suppose," said the King crossly. "Bless you, my children."

He was less cross when it was explained to him that the apprentice was really the Prince of the Fortunate Islands, and a much better match than the Prince of the Diamond Mountains, and he was quite in a good temper by the time the nurse threw herself in front of the throne and begged the King to let the Magician off altogether—chiefly on the ground that when he was a baby he was the dearest little duck that ever was, in the prettiest plaid frock, with the loveliest fat legs.

The King, moved by these arguments, said:

"I'll spare him if he'll promise to be good."

"You will, ducky, won't you?" said the nurse, crying.

"No," said the Magician, "I won't; and what's more, I can't."

The Princess, who was now so happy that she wanted everyone else to be happy too, begged her lover to make Taykin good "by magic".

"Alas, my dearest lady," said the Prince, "no one can be made good by magic. I could take the badness out of him—there's an excellent recipe in this note-book—but if I did that there'd be so little left."

"Every little helps," said the nurse wildly.

Prince Fortunatus, who was James, who was the apprentice, studied the book for a few moments, and then said a few words in a language no one present had ever heard before.

And as he spoke the wicked Magician began to tremble and shrink.

"Oh, my boy—be good! Promise you'll be good," cried the nurse still in tears.

The Magician seemed to be shrinking inside his clothes. He grew smaller and smaller. The nurse caught him in her arms, and still he grew less and less, till she seemed to be holding nothing but a bundle of clothes. Then with a cry of love and triumph she tore the Magician's clothes away and held up a chubby baby boy, with the very plaid frock and fat legs she had so often and so lovingly described.

"I said there wouldn't be much of him when his badness was out," said the Prince Fortunatus.

"I will be good; oh, I will," said the baby boy that had been the Magician.

"I'll see to that," said the nurse. And so the story ends with love and a wedding, and showers of white roses.

The Elephant's Child

In the High and Far-Off Times the Elephant, O Best Beloved, had no trunk. He had only a blackish, bulgy nose, as big as a boot, that he could wriggle about from side to side; but he couldn't pick up things with it. But there was one Elephant— a new Elephant—an Elephant's Child—who was full of 'satiable curtiosity, and that means he asked ever so many questions. And he lived in Africa, and he filled all Africa with his 'satiable curtiosities. He asked his tall aunt, the Ostrich, why her tail-feathers grew just so, and his tall aunt, the Ostrich, spanked him with her hard, hard claw. He asked his tall uncle, the Giraffe, what made his skin spotty, and his tall uncle, the Giraffe, spanked him with his hard, hard hoof. And still he was full of 'satiable curtiosity! He asked his broad aunt, the Hippopotamus, why her eyes were red, and his broad aunt, the Hippopotamus, spanked him with her broad, broad hoof; and he asked his hairy uncle, the Baboon, why melons tasted just so, and his hairy uncle, the Baboon, spanked him with his hairy, hairy paw. And still he was full of 'satiable curtiosity! He asked questions about everything that he saw, or heard, or felt, or smelt, or touched, and all his uncles and aunts spanked him. And still he was full of 'satiable curtiosity!

One fine morning in the middle of the Precession of the Equinoxes this 'satiable Elephant's Child asked a new fine question that he had never asked before. He asked, "What does the Crocodile have for dinner?" Then everybody said, "Hush!"

in a loud and dretful tone, and they spanked him immediately and directly, without stopping, for a long time.

By and by, when that was finished, he came upon Kolokolo Bird sitting in the middle of a wait-a-bit thorn-bush, and he said, "My father has spanked me, and my mother has spanked me; all my aunts and uncles have spanked me for my 'satiable curtiosity; and still I want to know what the Crocodile has for dinner!"

Then the Kolokolo Bird said, with a mournful cry, "Go to the banks of the great, grey-green, greasy Limpopo River, all set about with fever-trees, and find out."

That very next morning, when there was nothing left of the Equinoxes, because the Precession had preceded according to precedent, this 'satiable Elephant's Child took a hundred pounds of sugar-cane (the long purple kind), and seventeen melons (the greeny-crackly kind), and said to all his dear families, "Good-bye. I am going to the great, grey-green, greasy Limpopo River, all set about with fever-trees, to find out what the Crocodile has for dinner." And they all spanked him once more for luck, though he asked them most politely to stop.

Then he went away, a little warm, but not at all astonished, eating melons, and throwing the rind about, because he could not pick it up.

He went from Graham's Town to Kimberley, and from Kimberley to Khama's Country, and from Khama's Country he went east by north, eating melons all the time, till at last he came to the banks of the great, grey-green, greasy Limpopo River, all set about with fever-trees, precisely as Kolokolo Bird had said.

Now you must know and understand, O Best Beloved, that till that very week, and day, and hour, and minute, this 'satiable Elephant's Child had never seen a Crocodile, and did not know what one was like. It was all his 'satiable curtiosity.

The first thing he found was a Bi-Coloured-Python-Rock-Snake, curled round a rock.

"'Scuse me," said the Elephant's Child most politely, "but have you seen such a thing as a Crocodile in these promiscuous parts?"

"Have I seen a Crocodile?" said the Bi-Coloured-Python-Rock-Snake, in a voice of dretful scorn. "What will you ask me next?"

"'Scuse me," said the Elephant's Child, "but could you kindly tell me what he has for dinner?"

Then the Bi-Coloured-Python-Rock-Snake uncoiled himself very quickly from the rock, and spanked the Elephant's Child with his scalesome, flailsome tail.

"That is odd," said the Elephant's Child, "because my father and my mother, and my uncle and my aunt, not to mention my other aunt, the Hippopotamus, and my other uncle, the Baboon, have all spanked me for my 'satiable curtiosity—and I suppose this is the same thing."

So he said good-bye very politely to the Bi-Coloured-Python-Rock-Snake, and helped to coil him up on the rock again, and went on, a little warm, but not at all astonished, eating melons, and throwing the rind about, because he could not pick it up, till he trod on what he thought was a log of wood at the very edge of the great, grey-green, greasy Limpopo River, all set about with fever-trees.

But it was really the Crocodile, O Best Beloved, and the Crocodile winked one eye—like this!

"'Scuse me," said the Elephant's Child most politely, "but do you happen to have seen a Crocodile in these promiscuous parts?"

Then the Crocodile winked the other eye, and lifted half his tail out of the mud; and the Elephant's Child stepped back most politely, because he did not wish to be spanked again.

"Come hither, Little One," said the Crocodile. "Why do you ask such things?"

"'Scuse me," said the Elephant's Child most politely, "but my father has spanked me, my mother has spanked me, not to mention my tall aunt, the Ostrich, and my tall uncle, the Giraffe who can kick ever so hard, as well as my broad aunt, the Hippopotamus, and my hairy uncle, the Baboon, and including the Bi-Coloured-Python-Rock-Snake, with the scalesome, flailsome tail, just up the bank, who spanks harder than any of them; and so, if it's quite all the same to you, I don't want to be spanked any more."

"Come hither, Little One," said the Crocodile, "for I am the Crocodile," and he wept crocodile-tears to show it was quite true.

Then the Elephant's Child grew all breathless, and panted, and kneeled down on the bank and said, "You are the very person I have been looking for all these long days. Will you please tell me what you have for dinner?"

"Come hither, Little One," said the Crocodile, "and I'll whisper."

Then the Elephant's Child put his head down close to the Crocodile's musky, tusky mouth, and the Crocodile caught him by his little nose, which up to that very week, day, hour, and minute, had been no bigger than a boot, though much more useful.

"I think," said the Crocodile—and he said it between his teeth, like this—"I think today I will begin with Elephant's Child!"

At this, O Best Beloved, the Elephant's Child was much annoyed, and he said, speaking through his nose, like this, "Led go! You are hurtig be!"

Then the Bi-Coloured-Python-Rock-Snake scuffed down from the bank and said, "My young friend, if you do not now, immediately and instantly, pull as hard as ever you can, it is my opinion that your acquaintance in the large-pattern leather ulster" (and by this he meant the Crocodile) "will jerk you into yonder limpid stream before you can say Jack Robinson."

This is the way Bi-Coloured-Python-Rock-Snakes always talk.

Then the Elephant's Child sat back on his little haunches, and pulled, and pulled, and his nose began to stretch. And the Crocodile floundered into the water, making it all creamy with great sweeps of his tail, and he pulled, and pulled, and pulled.

And the Elephant's Child's nose kept on stretching; and the Elephant's Child spread all his little four legs and pulled, and pulled, and pulled, and his nose kept on stretching; and the Crocodile threshed his tail like an oar, and he pulled, and pulled, and pulled, and at each pull the Elephant's Child's nose grew longer and longer—and it hurt him hijjus!

Then the Elephant's Child felt his legs slipping, and he said through his nose, which was now nearly five feet long, "This is too butch for be!"

Then the Bi-Coloured-Python-Rock-Snake came down from the bank, and knotted himself in a double-clove-hitch round the Elephant's Child's hind-legs, and said, "Rash and inexperienced traveller, we will now seriously devote ourselves to a little high tension, because if we do not, it is my impression that yonder self-propelling man-of-war with the armour-plated upper deck" (and by this, O Best ·Beloved, he meant the Crocodile) "will permanently vitiate your future career."

That is the way all Bi-Coloured-Python-Rock-Snakes always talk.

So he pulled, and the Elephant's Child pulled, and the Crocodile pulled; but the Elephant's Child and the Bi-Coloured-Python-Rock-Snake pulled hardest; and at last the Crocodile let go of the Elephant's Child's nose with a plop that you could hear all up and down the Limpopo.

Then the Elephant's Child sat down most hard and sudden; but first he was careful to say "Thank you" to the Bi-Coloured-Python-Rock-Snake; and next he was kind to his poor pulled nose, and wrapped it all up in cool banana leaves, and hung it in the great, grey-green, greasy Limpopo to cool.

"What are you doing that for?" said the Bi-Coloured-Python-Rock-Snake.

"'Scuse me," said the Elephant's Child, "but my nose is badly out of shape, and I am waiting for it to shrink."

"Then you will have to wait a long time," said the Bi-Coloured-Python-Rock-Snake. "Some people do not know what is good for them."

The Elephant's Child sat there for three days waiting for his nose to shrink. But it never grew any shorter, and, besides, it made him squint. For, O Best Beloved, you will see and understand that the Crocodile had pulled it out into a really truly trunk same as all Elephants have today.

At the end of the third day a fly came and stung him on the shoulder, and before he knew what he was doing he lifted up his trunk and hit that fly dead with the end of it.

"Vantage number one!" said the Bi-Coloured-Python-Rock-Snake. "You couldn't have done that with a mere-smear nose. Try and eat a little now."

Before he thought what he was doing the Elephant's Child put out his trunk and plucked a large bundle of grass, dusted it clean against his fore-legs, and stuffed it into his own mouth.

"Vantage number two!" said the Bi-Coloured-Python-Rock-Snake. "You couldn't have done that with a mere-smear nose. Don't you think the sun is very hot here?"

"It is," said the Elephant's Child, and before he thought what he was doing he schlooped up a schloop of mud from the banks of the great, grey-green, greasy Limpopo, and slapped it on his head, where it made a cool schloopy-sloshy mud-cap all trickly behind his ears.

"Vantage number three!" said the Bi-Coloured-Python-Rock-Snake. "You couldn't have done that with a mere-smear nose. Now how do you feel about being spanked again?"

"'Scuse me," said the Elephant's Child, "but I should not like it at all."

"How would you like to spank somebody?" said the Bi-Coloured-Python-Rock-Snake.

"I should like it very much indeed," said the Elephant's Child.

"Well," said the Bi-Coloured-Python-Rock-Snake, "you will find that new nose of yours very useful to spank people with."

"Thank you," said the Elephant's Child, "I'll remember that; and now I think I'll go home to all my dear families and try."

So the Elephant's Child went home across Africa frisking and whisking his trunk. When he wanted fruit to eat he pulled fruit down from a tree, instead of waiting for it to fall as he used to do. When he wanted grass he plucked grass up from the ground, instead of going on his knees as he used to do. When the flies bit him he broke off the branch of a tree and used it as a fly-whisk; and he made himself a new, cool, slushy-squshy mud-cap whenever the sun was hot. When he felt lonely walking through

Africa he sang to himself down his trunk, and the noise was louder than several brass bands. He went specially out of his way to find a broad Hippopotamus (she was no relation of his), and he spanked her very hard, to make sure that the Bi-Coloured-Python-Rock-Snake had spoken the truth about his new trunk. The rest of the time he picked up the melon-rinds that he had dropped on his way to the Limpopo—for he was a Tidy Pachyderm.

One dark evening he came back to all his dear families, and he coiled up his trunk and said, "How do you do?" They were very glad to see him, and immediately said "Come here and be spanked for your 'satiable curtiosity."

"Pooh," said the Elephant's Child. "I don't think you peoples know anything about spanking; but I do, and I'll show you."

Then he uncurled his trunk and knocked two of his dear brothers head over heels.

"O Bananas!" said they, "where did you learn that trick, and what have you done to your nose?"

"I got a new one from the Crocodile on the banks of the great, grey-green, greasy Limpopo River," said the Elephant's Child. "I asked him what he had for dinner, and he gave me this to keep."

"It looks very ugly," said his hairy uncle, the Baboon.

"It does," said the Elephant's Child. "But it's very useful," and he picked up his hairy uncle, the Baboon, by one hairy leg, and hove him into a hornet's nest.

Then that bad Elephant's Child spanked all his dear families for a long time, till they were very warm and greatly astonished. He pulled out his tall Ostrich aunt's tail-feathers; and he caught his tall uncle, the Giraffe, by the hind-leg, and dragged him through a thorn-bush; and he shouted at his broad aunt, the Hippopotamus, and blew bubbles into her ear when she was sleeping in the water after meals; but he never let any one touch Kolokolo Bird.

The Elephant's Child

At last things grew so exciting that his dear families went off one by one in a hurry to the banks of the great grey-green, greasy Limpopo River, all set about with fever-trees, to borrow new noses from the Crocodile. When they came back nobody spanked anybody any more, and ever since that day, O Best Beloved, all the Elephants you will ever see, besides all those that you won't, have trunks precisely like the trunk of the 'satiable Elephant's Child.